FOREST
Presented by The Writing Tree

Forest
First published in 2018
by Writing Tree Press

All rights reserved. No part of this publication may be reproduced, stored in a database or retrieval system, or transmitted, in any form or by any means, without the prior permission in writing of the publisher, nor be otherwise circulated in any form or binding or cover other than that in which it is published and without a similar condition including this condition being imposed on the subsequent purchaser.

© 2018 respective authors
Cover art © 2018 by RainDragon Arts

The moral rights of the authors have been asserted.
All characters and events in this publication, other than those clearly in the pubic domain, are fictitious, and any resemblance to any real person, living or dead, is purely coincidental and not intended by the authors.

ISBN: 978-1-9999757-2-2

For information contact:
Writing Tree Press, Unit 10773, PO Box 4336
Manchester, M61 0BW
www.writingtree.co.uk

Dedication

*For all the creators out there
who do their thing for the love of it,
and generously share it with the rest of us.*

Contents

Foreword	1
Season	3
Smoke: A Women Of White Water Story	4
Woodless	33
Petr, Husband Of Fevronia	39
The Gift	65
For The Trees	75
Wild	104
Razorback	109
Land Of Make Believe	136
About The Contributors	155
About The Writing Tree	158
Acknowledgements	159

Foreword

It's fitting that this collection of stories (and the poem that introduces them) is the first publication by the Writing Tree Press. I began the Writing Tree thinking it would be something I could do in a small way to help others get the pleasure from writing that I do. Then times got dark, and it fell by the wayside; it felt like an impossible dream. As they always do, though, my friends stepped in to support me when life knocked me down. They picked me up, dusted me off, and we went forwards together. What had been a lone tree became a wood. A forest. An ecosystem of friendship and creativity. However far apart or close we may be geographically, we communicate just as the trees do, our roots gently tickling the earth. Or, you know, talking on WhatsApp, because trees are far more advanced than we are on the earth-tickling front.

For over ten years we have been meeting every year for a summer writing retreat, and two years ago we formed a writing group, online and at cake-fuelled meetings in my house, to keep us going in between. There's been a lot of laughter, shameless fangirling and endless discussions of semicolons, participles of all kinds, and why dragons and werewolves make most things better.

It is with pride and love that I present for your reading pleasure these stories from a bunch of my favourite writers. You'll find romance, horror, mystery and a lot of trees in this book. I hope you enjoy the ride as much as we have.

Helen Kenwright
January, 2018

Season
by Susi Liarte

I don't want to be parted from the open sky
I walk the path regardless, abandoning the light
The shade of boughs is dark and wild in its embrace
The humid air that greets me leaves an unknown taste

The thorns of my invention give way to gentle flowers
I watch the leaves unfurling, a season in an hour
The ground alive beneath me forgives me as I stride
I'm leaving footprint kisses, the shadows now my guide

The day is stark above us and the forest listens
Naked branches reaching with black bone fingers
A new year will bring dark-sown seeds in a waking soil
Until then I will yearn for the canopy
When the last leaf falls

Smoke:
a Women of White Water Story
by Helen Kenwright

Berta let herself in through Andrea's front door, hung up her coat and popped her umbrella in the trendy umbrella stand in the corner of the hall. The stand collected rainwater and channelled it to water a planter nearby. The planter contained a creeping fig that twisted itself around the wire frame of the hall mirror. It all seemed unnecessarily complicated to Berta, but she did like a bit of indoor greenery.

Andrea was in her living room, sitting at the dining room table and staring at her laptop screen.

"Good afternoon," said Berta. "Bit damp out."

Andrea glanced up. "Mmm?"

"The weather. Bit damp." Berta waved in the direction of the patio doors, which were speckled with rain drops. "Is that your washing out there?"

"Oh, yeah. I forgot."

Berta rushed to the rescue, grabbing the wicker laundry basket from the airing cupboard as she went. She was just in time: the clothes were damp but not yet soaked. She snapped off pegs and caught the falling laundry neatly in the basket. The last sock dropped in just as the rain kicked up a notch and went from damp to full-on soaking.

"That was quick," said Andrea. "Thanks."

"You should keep a closer eye on things. This weather's due to settle in for a few days. Things never dry as well on the airer."

"I'd forgotten it was out there, to be honest. Got a

bit wrapped up in work."

"Yes, well. I'll start folding, you get the kettle on, girl."

Berta hummed to herself as she folded laundry from the basket into neat piles on Andrea's living room table. Andrea's clothes were a novelty, very different from her own. Mostly white and cream with accents of lilac and turquoise. Crisp cotton, soft linen. Berta's clothes were all the colours of the rainbow, cut for comfort and coverage. Andrea dressed as if she wished she were a cloud.

She was a quarter of a century younger than Berta, though. She probably still cared what she looked like.

"It happened again yesterday," Andrea said. She hadn't shifted from her place at the other end of the table. "Smoke in the sky over Neverhulme."

"Probably a dark cloud," said Berta. "Doubt they'd notice the difference. It's like dealing with people from the dark ages."

"Are you still bearing a grudge? They're just a bit rigid in their thinking, that's all."

"It's rude to ask a Wise Woman where her Knowledge comes from. All that rubbish about the subconscious observation of micro-communication. As if magic wasn't a perfectly rational explanation."

"They're happy enough to listen to what you Know."

"Of course. They'd be fools not to."

Berta would never admit it, but those questions had rattled her. Naturally, she'd been curious as to how she came by her power, especially when she was Andrea's age. She remembered asking her grandmother why other people couldn't sense truths like she could.

Grana had asked her if she needed to know why some people could tell when a storm was coming, or what the sex of an unborn baby was, or could do sums really fast in their head. 'Life's too short to question everything,' Grana had said. 'Best be selective, or there won't be time to do anything with the answers.'

"Berta?" said Andrea. "I said, will you go and talk to them?"

"I will not help unless asked," said Berta, stiffly. "And if they sent me an invitation it was clearly lost in the post."

"I could go," said Andrea.

"You will not."

Andrea sighed.

"This sock needs darning," said Berta, irritably.

Andrea murmured something and directed her attention back at her laptop.

"We're not heroes," said Berta. "We're-"

"'Just people with a talent', yes, I know."

"No better than anyone else," said Berta.

Andrea gave her a long, narrow-eyed look. Berta bristled. She patted the top of the pile of folded laundry. "Nearly dry. Won't need more than a flick of an iron."

Andrea's expression softened. "Thank you."

"Yes. Well. I-"

Andrea's gaze had already drifted back to her screen.

"Very well," said Berta. "Good day."

She swept out, tucking the sock into her pocket as she went.

Berta sipped her tea. She murmured appreciatively; the lavender honey wasn't overly sweet, but brought out the cloves nicely. "Another winner, Sunita. I don't know what you do with those bees of yours, but it works."

Sunita smiled, and offered the teapot for Berta to

help herself to a top-up. "So, do you think you'll go and investigate this business in the forest?"

"Oh, no."

Sunita raised an eyebrow.

"I really haven't the time. The Carters are in all sorts of trouble with their mother. It's going to take quite some sorting out."

"She's not gambling again, I hope?

"Hard to say. She won't come to see me, and there's only so much I can do with the rest of the family. They're all so volatile, what with Stuart and the baby and now his sister's kicking up a fuss about the football team. So I think the forest will have to fend for itself."

"And Andrea?"

Berta twisted the lid of the teapot around so the ornate, swirling pattern lined up. "She's very busy with her accountancy."

"Berta-"

"Very busy."

"You've brought her on so well. Don't you think she's ready?"

Berta rested her cup in its saucer. "Ready for what, exactly?"

"Forgive me. It's none of my business, my dear."

"I began my apprenticeship the minute I was born. Andrea's only been with me for eighteen months, and she has some very modern ideas."

"Didn't you, once upon a time? I remember your grandmother coming through that very door, all hot and flustered, ranting to my father for a full half hour about how impossible you were." Sunita leaned forwards conspiratorially. "I used to hide in the larder to listen. Even those of us without talent can learn secrets."

"I wish you'd all do it more often. It would be nice to take a day off, once in a while."

There was an uneasy sensation in Berta's stomach. A flutter of uncertainty. Berta was used to being right. Partly because, thanks to the gift of Knowing what was in peoples' hearts, she usually was. Partly because, as Grana used to say, she was an obstinate person with an underdeveloped sense of her own fallibility. 'You're a proper little Know-it-all,' Grana would say, and they'd both laugh at the pun and Grana would forget what she'd been telling Berta off for.

"It's never easy to let go," Sunita said. She took Berta's hand and looked into her eyes. The river rushed: white, foamy waves speckled with gold, and Berta Knew.

Berta pulled her hand back and nursed it in her lap, stroking her knuckles back and forth. "That's not right, Sunita."

"It seemed like the best way to explain what I meant."

"It's not like that. It's not telepathy. You have no idea!" Berta's heart raced.

"I have nothing to hide, Berta. And everything to give."

Berta closed her eyes for a moment. She could smell the cinnamon biscuits on the plate between them; she could hear the tinkling of the little bells threaded through the trees in the garden outside. Sunita was the sparkle of the river, the caress of the water around the biggest boulders. Sunita was....

"Andrea is not my child. And I am not a mother. You are riddled with fear that you did the wrong thing: that you let your children flee the nest too early, too late, too boldly, too timidly. Your heart is a swarming nest of maternal uncertainty and loneliness. You miss your brothers. You miss your children. Your bees are your children now. And you feel sorry for me, because I never knew the pleasure of nursing a babe."

Berta watched Sunita's face cool and harden. A fragment of understanding passed between them before her protections were back in place.

"It's not like that," she said, her voice wavering. "It's more complicated than you-"

"No. It's not. I had better be going."

"Berta, I'm sorry. I didn't wish to offend you."

"I know." Berta got to her feet. She picked up the shawl she'd draped over the back of the chair and pulled it around her shoulders. "Every mother feels the same, Sunita. When you love with all your heart, nothing is ever enough. But you are a good mother, and your children are a credit to you. Good morning."

Andrea chose her usual table at the cafe and took a long look at the menu. Reading was soothing. It kept her ordered, logical mind to the fore, and left the emotions to seethe around by themselves in the background where they couldn't spoil her day.

She breathed in the smell of damp coats and coffee mixed with cinnamon and chocolate. The windows were steamed up, creating a cosy, warm little bubble away from the world.

The kitchen door swung open and Matt emerged. He noticed Andrea straight away.

"Are you all right, lovie?" he said. "I was starting to worry you'd been swept away in the deluge."

"It's only a spring shower," said Andrea. As if to prove her wrong, the rain started to beat against the window like a kettle drum.

"So, Yorkshire 'cino? How about an almond flaky bun? There's a fresh batch just come out of the oven."

"Yes," said Andrea. "Oh God, yes."

Matt smiled at her and whisked out his cloth to give the table a wipe, although to Andrea's eye it was perfectly clean already. "You just relax, lovie. I'll be right back."

Andrea got her laptop out as soon as he'd gone. The excuse she gave herself was that she needed to check her notes for that afternoon's vid-meet with Craig from the Leeds office, but of course she went straight back to the notes she'd started on Neverhulme. The smoke. The rumours. The rushing of the river in her mind.

Andrea sighed. It had been over a year now, and the Knowing still had the power to disconcert her. She envied how unbothered Berta was by it. It was just part of her, a sense like any other. For Andrea it was like a burst of morning sun in her eyes, a splash of cold water to the face. It was raw and unfocused. It had taken her months before she could make any sense of it at all. Even now, where Berta saw into peoples' hearts with a sharp, certain clarity, Andrea saw only unease and distress, with the occasional hint of a truth. But Andrea had something else, something she suspected Berta did not. She could sense wrongness at a different level. Where Berta saw depths of the individual soul, Andrea saw the bonds between people. She saw the colony, not the ant. She supposed eventually, as she practised, she'd hone it down to the person. And then she could be more use: communities did not really care for advice in the way that individuals did.

There was something niggling at her about Neverhulme.

A cup of coffee arrived on her table, along with a pastry on a blue and white plate with a little fork, and a soft, linen napkin.

Andrea felt better just looking at it.

"Can I join you?" Matt said. "Sadie said I can take my break early."

Andrea pulled out the chair next to her. "Help

yourself."

"I've had a 'mare of a morning. The toaster's broken again and it was Sadie's late start. What's up with yours?"

"Nothing." Andrea put a forkful of almond heaven into her mouth.

"If you say so." Matt straightened the menu rack.

"Berta. She's incapable of accepting any idea if she didn't think of it first."

"You've been having ideas? That's a bit rash."

"It's not funny. I want to learn, that's all."

"Sorry. Tell me your ideas."

"I have this... Feeling. About Neverhulme."

"Oh, the scary smoke? I heard they're talking about patrols. Smoke in the forest isn't a good sign, even in this weather."

"Exactly! So we should investigate, right?"

"We?"

"Berta and I. Or, well, Berta, I suppose."

"Oh, right. They asked?"

"Not exactly. I mean, they might have, but you know how Berta is."

Matt lined up the salt and pepper pots behind the menu rack.

Andrea finished her pastry, and took a sip of her coffee. "I'm not a kid," she said. "I'm thirty next year. And I didn't ask for this... whatever it is."

"I know, lovie," said Matt. "But you're going to be damn good at it, all the same."

Berta walked briskly, trying not to notice the thoughts racing through her mind at a million miles an hour. Instead she deliberately turned her ear to the birds, her eye to the grey, clammy sky. Real things. Things that were blessedly none of her concern, and required nothing of her to exist. She was headed for home. The little cottage buried in the hillside up by North Street, where there would be a warm fire and cosy slippers and a nice cup of tea. But instead her feet took her to the café in Market Street, where Andrea was sitting with her friend Matt and a cup of something disgusting covered in foam.

"Good afternoon," said Berta. "You should go to the forest. If you like. Soon. I expect."

Andrea blinked at her.

"Right." She glanced at Matt. "Seeing as I'm here, I'll have a scone."

"What?" said Andrea. "Sorry, did you just say--"

"I'm far too busy. It's probably nothing. You should go. Scone, please. Jam and butter, no cream."

"'Course." Matt sprang to his feet and went to the kitchen. Berta sat herself down in the seat he'd just vacated.

"Why did you change your mind?" said Andrea.

Berta considered, or at least her face did. The rest of her tried to process what she'd just done.

"First rule," she said. "You will not make a spreadsheet of this."

"Of course not," said Andrea. And then, "Why?"

"Because Knowing is an art, not a science. You feel it. You don't plan it."

Andrea frowned. Berta sympathised. She could do with a plan herself right now. This was uncharted territory.

"It's a test. There's rules. You know, Guild nonsense. I'll email them to you."

"Thanks. Is there any kind of brief? Normally there's a client and they have questions and... Is there a client? Did someone ask you?"

"Strictly speaking, no. You can call me the client if it makes you feel better."

"I'm not sure it does."

"No, well. Sometimes we do things because we see a problem. Something as needs fixing. And you did. That Neverhulme business. So you go fix it."

"Without permission."

"Of course not without permission, silly girl."

Andrea took a deep breath. It occurred to Berta that she was probably making a mess of this.

Matt arrived with a glass of raspberry cordial and a fat, fluffy scone.

"Thank you," said Berta.

"Matt has a friend who lives in Neverhulme," said Andrea.

"I do?" said Matt, popping Andrea's empty plate on his tray.

"That boy you like."

"Orchid? He's not exactly a boyfriend.

"You were talking to him at ceramics class on Tuesday."

"That hardly makes him my-"

Andrea gave him a look. Andrea's looks could be very penetrating sometimes. Berta put it down to accountancy.

"He was in charge of the kiln," Matt muttered, looking down at his tray. "We may have exchanged a few words."

"About Neverhulme?"

"He was worried about the smoke. What's going on?"

Andrea leaned back in her chair, and folded her arms across her chest. "Worrying is a considerable threat to wellbeing, isn't it, Berta?"

"It would be kind to check he's all right," said Berta, barely restraining the urge to beam with pride.

The path to Neverhulme went north from the crossroads on the other side of the bridge from White Water, winding away from the river and into the forest on the far bank. The trees were flushed with bright new leaves against a backdrop of enduring evergreen. The path was thick with mulch, slippery in places. Berta placed her feet with all the confidence of a woman wearing a really sturdy pair of boots, but Andrea was more cautious. She didn't walk much. Preferred her bicycle. That's young people for you. Always in a rush.

"Any questions?" Berta asked.

"I don't think so."

"You sent off the forms?"

Andrea gave her a thunderous look. Fair enough. The girl had never failed to complete paperwork in her life.

"I thought we could start with Matt's friend, Orchid," Andrea said. "He seems nice."

"That would be a first," said Berta. "For your friend Matt to pick a pleasant object for his affections."

"He made some lovely bathroom tiles the other week," said Andrea, fiddling with a loose thread in the thumb of her glove. "They had seahorses on."

"That's appropriate for bathrooms, I suppose."

"They're for his aunt, he said. According to Matt. I mean, I see him every week. He's not likely to throw us out, at least. He's a performer, so he knows a lot of people."

"Trust your instincts. There's no need to fret."

"I'm not fretting."

Berta patted her arm. "Come along. The days are short in the forest. I'd like to be done and dusted by tea time."

The entrance to Neverhulme was an ostentatious fence, taller than a person, with a double-doored gate in it. The fence and gate were made of thick wooden slats, carved to a point at the tops. It was completely unnecessary: it wasn't as if there were a threat of barbarian hordes, and even if there were, all they'd need was a little flame and the whole lot would go up. Berta supposed it was an image thing.

"Here we are, then," she said to Andrea. "In you go. I'll meet you back here at about four."

"What?"

"I'm on cleaning rota at the village hall. Besides, that gives you over eight hours. Shouldn't think it'll take you that long. If you finish early, send a message. I'll try and remember to keep the thing on." She patted her right coat pocket, where she kept her device. She was fairly sure she'd left it on the windowsill to charge yesterday. If not, well, Andrea would cope. She was very capable. Intelligent.

She was looking at Berta like a lost orphan. Oh, in the name of the river and all the sacred earth.

"Good luck," said Berta. "Try not to mention magic."

She gave Andrea an impulsive hug, and walked away.

Andrea thought about storming off, but she didn't have a chance to act on it before the gates swung open. A man wearing a woolly hat with a peak and ear flaps thrust a clipboard into her hands. "Morning. Sign in please. I'll get you a visitor's band."

Andrea looked down at the clipboard. There was a single sheet of paper on it, bearing a table headed 'name', 'purpose of visit', 'arrival time' and 'departure time'. There was a pencil attached to the board with a tatty bit of string. She obediently filled in her details. Under 'purpose of visit' she wrote 'book-keeping consultation' because it made her feel more like herself.

"Grand. Here y'go." The gatekeeper exchanged the clipboard for a woven bracelet. It had the word 'visitor' embroidered on it in luminous green thread. "Have a nice day."

"Thanks."

Andrea straightened her shoulders, and headed for the village square ahead.

The people of Neverhulme were primarily foresters and woodcrafters, with a sprinkling of artists and engineers. They traded for any food the forest didn't provide, generated their own energy from the solar leaves wound through the trees they lived in, and paid taxes to Leeds for networked utilities. The buildings at Neverhulme blended with the forest, rather than being built despite it. Branches formed beams to support roofs; trunks formed walls. Planks cut from deadwood and careful forestry linked the lives of people and the lives of the trees. But as communities went, they were less connected than most. Forest dwelling wasn't for everyone.

Andrea had to admit there was something romantic about the tree-houses, though: the rope bridge walk ways and the twinkling fairy lights that adorned all the populated trees. At ground level there was a circle of logs around a heating dome, which would glow warm at night, giving warmth and light to all who clustered around it. The great storyteller Stenolf lived here, when he wasn't travelling the old roads of Yorkshire, exchanging stories for a bed for the night. He'd come to White Water last spring and captivated the whole village with tales of the days before the Cataclysm. Days of greed and grime, he'd called them. The phrase stuck in Andrea's head for days, sending a fresh shiver down her spine every time she recalled it.

Today the circle was quiet, apart from a few customers wandering around the stalls that formed its perimeter. Food smells drifted across to Andrea: fresh bread, stew, spiced apples, all against a backdrop of bark and leaves, pine and cedar. She took a moment to enjoy the thought that Berta would have loved it. Spiced apples were her favourite.

Served her right she was missing out.

The community was strong here. Andrea shut her eyes and sensed golden threads connecting families, friends, the traders and the craftspeople and the trees. But there was one space that echoed with the snap of brittle fractures. Andrea's eyes were drawn to a large cabin that stood beyond the circle. The meeting place of the Elders.

Best start there, then.

Berta pulled her shawl a little tighter around her shoulders, and plodded on into the heart of the forest. A stream began here, bubbling out of the ground and dancing towards the river. Over the years it had cut into the earth, made the ground thick with water and washed the tree roots bare. The trees didn't seem to mind. They simply burrowed deeper into the earth and enjoyed the nutrients the stream brought their way.

A little while later, Berta came across a hole in the ground. It was small, just barely big enough for a person to drop through. Providing the person was thin and limber. If a thin, limber person - such as Berta had once been herself - were to drop into the hole, they would find a path leading underground, down old tunnels carved by old rivers, and among them glittering caves. Limestone to a river is like a lump of clay to a potter. Raw material, begging to be moulded and cut into something more interesting.

The hole was covered by a dome of woven branches these days, painted red to show the unwary traveller that it would be a very bad idea to have anything to do with it. It was circled by hawthorn and holly. Around it were footprints imprinted in the soft, bare earth. Berta could cover them entirely with hers.

The footprints came from the direction of

Neverhulme; Berta had been idly following them for some time. But there were none moving away from the hole. There were scratches through the ground where the dome had been pulled back into place.

Someone was in the hole.

Berta looked around.

She spotted a pile of logs on the edge of the clearing up ahead. She fetched one, brushed off the worst of the dirt with a sleeve tugged over the back of her hand, and sat. She kicked the dome away from the hole.

"Good afternoon," she said.

There was the faintest of rustlings from inside the hole. It could, perhaps, be a rabbit.

It wasn't a rabbit.

The meeting of the Elders of Neverhulme was beginning as Andrea joined the villagers on the scrutiny benches. Neverhulme was known throughout Yorkshire for the quality of its dyes, made in big vats from the leaves and roots of plants. The villagers wore their craft with pride, especially the Elders, as their most respected citizens. They wore cloaks of vibrant pink over shirts and trousers of green and purple.

"As lives the forest, so live the people of Neverhulme," said the Eldermost. "Those who live longest and grow strongest are the canopy that shelters the community. Under our protection diversity flourishes, all have their place in the circle of life and death and rebirth. We see the old leaves fall and the new shoots rise. May all under the canopy bear fruit!"

"May all bear fruit," answered the ten other elders. They raised cups of water to the sky as if by way of a toast, then drank.

"We have much to discuss," the Eldermost said.

"Pass the wyrmrod and speak your concerns."

The Eldermost produced a wand, around which curled an ornately carved dragon. It was passed to the Elder to the left, a woman with steely grey hair and bright, piercing eyes. She set it on the table in front of her, and touched the dragon's head with her fingertips.

"I raise before the Elders of Neverhulme the question of the smoke seen to the East," she said. "Why have no parties of inquiry been sent to investigate?"

"Elder Belmarsh," said the Eldermost. "This was your duty, was it not?"

"It was, and I fulfilled it. I told you yesterday. There was nothing."

The woman with the wyrmrod regarded her fellow Elder with a cynical expression.

"There were no ashes," said Belmarsh. "It must have been a freak weather phenomena. Or something of that nature."

All Elders looked at Belmarsh, who fidgeted with his cup and kept his eyes down. He was clearly lying.

"I suggest we open a further party of enquiry," said the woman with the wyrmrod. "One that actually knows what it's doing."

Murmurs of agreement came from around the table and the villagers sitting around Andrea. The river tumbled and twisted through her mind.

"Elder Belmarsh-" the Eldermost began.

"There's really no need!" Belmarsh blurted out. "No harm was done. The forest is well. It was a freak of nature. I urge you all, please, let us move to more serious matters."

"Elder Belmarsh must be deluded," said another Elder. He wore a scarf in the most vibrant shade of orange Andrea had ever seen. "Not for the first time." A few sniggers broke out among the villagers, and the orange-scarfed Elder smirked. "But this particular delusion is dangerous to us all. Has he perhaps forgotten that fire is our deadliest enemy?"

"You insult me!" Belmarsh shouted. "I shall listen to no more of this!"

With that he leapt to his feet stormed out of the cabin. The villagers stared in amazement and a couple of the Elders stood up and turned to the door, as if to follow him.

"Let him go," the Eldermost said. "Elder Harrison, will you lead a new party of enquiry into the event of the smoke?"

"But, Eldermost," said the woman with the wyrmrod.

The Eldermost looked straight at Andrea, and said, "Fear not, Elder Spencer. I believe our dear Elder Belmarsh will find the truth elsewhere."

Andrea raised an eyebrow; the Eldermost gave her the slightest smile, the merest nod.

"Very well," said Elder Spencer, who appeared oblivious to the direction of the Eldermost's attention. "The reverend Eldermost will see to it that balance prevails."

The Elders drank again, and the wyrmrod was passed to the next Elder in the circle, and the next, and the next, until everyone had been offered the opportunity to speak. Then the meeting ended, and Andrea slipped out of the cabin and went in search of Belmarsh.

She found him sitting on a branch of an apple tree, swinging his legs for all the world as if he were a boy of ten, not a man of sixty or so. He would not have had to climb the tree, however: there was a rope ladder hanging down to the ground. Andrea caught herself just as she was about to call up to him to ask if it was all right to join him. Berta wouldn't ask. So instead Andrea took a deep breath, and placed her feet firmly, one after the other, on the ladder and pulled herself up the tree, into the cloud of blossom where he sat.

Belmarsh watched her curiously, as if she were an exotic beetle crawling over a leaf. She smiled politely and sat next to him. There were plump cushions tied to the branch, a row of three. She took the one closest to the trunk, leaving an empty station between the two of them. It was very high, now she was here. She tried not to think about that.

"It's all right," she said. "You're not in trouble about your credit record or anything."

"Aren't I?"

"Not as far as I'm aware."

"They can't have sent this month's tallies through yet, then. I owe everybody. It's going to be tough getting back to an even keel, especially when I resign from the council."

"Why should you resign from the council?"

"You heard them in there. They don't trust me. I'm disgraced."

"I wouldn't put it that strongly."

Belmarsh made a dismissive noise.

"You've always been well above balance. Not that it matters. I mean, I'm not here as an accountant today."

"I always prided myself on giving back more than I took from this community. Neverhulme means everything to me. The people, our culture, our way of living. The forest gave me life. I give back."

"So, what happened?"

"They say you have talent."

"Do they?"

"Like that Wise Woman. What's her name, Brenda?"

"Berta." Andrea could imagine the look on Berta's face if she knew they'd got her name wrong. She might save that up as revenge for Berta abandoning her here.

"Yeah, that's the one. You can see things."

"I have extreme empathic sensitivity. Of a sort."

"So you can read my mind?"

"No. If you consent, you can talk and I'll listen, and perhaps help you find some truths that would be useful for you. But I'm not as skilled as Berta. Not yet."

"No offence but if I wanted counselling I'd go to a counsellor."

Andrea's heart sank. This is exactly why Berta should be here. People didn't want someone who could tell them what they already knew, and Andrea was pretty sure Belmarsh was aware he was giving off an aura of desperation and fear. They wanted someone who could look in their hearts and tell them what they didn't know. The secrets they needed to face. A truth in a world of grey areas and dubious boundaries.

"What caused the smoke?" she asked.

Belmarsh's face went still and cold, mask-like. He didn't answer her.

She pushed. Partly because it's what Berta would expect, but also she found herself intensely curious. "You know, don't you?"

"Do I?"

"Yes, you-"

Andrea turned to him, trying to catch his gaze. But she'd forgotten she was sitting twenty feet up in a tree, not on a chair. She lost her balance for an instant and panic seized her; she was convinced she would fall. But Belmarsh caught her with a firm grip to her arm, pulling her back. The world stopped spinning and she felt safe, grounded. And then-

The river roared in her ears. She followed its flow as it cascaded down a valley, step after step.

Mist hovered over the splashing water, wispy like smoke, threaded with gold.

"It's your son," she said.

Belmarsh looked horrified. Andrea recognised the look. She'd seen it in so many of Berta's clients. But she hadn't stolen the truth from him. He'd given it to her.

"He took your credits," Andrea said.

"It's not his fault. It's the crowd he's been hanging around with. I should have been a better father."

"Yes, you should." A flicker of pain crossed his face. "Oh. Sorry. I'm still.... You're... It's hard to explain."

"It's all right." Belmarsh let go of her arm, slowly drawing his hand back. "You may as well get on with it."

"With what?"

"Telling the Council it's my son who caused the fire."

"Why would I do that?"

"It's all right. I give you my blessing to tell them. It'll be a relief, honestly, to get it out in the open."

"But it's not true."

Belmarsh's eyes narrowed.

"You think you believe it. It's fear, you see, it does that sometimes. You're all worked up because you dreaded something like this would happen. The Elders gossip about it. About him, about you. It hurts you very much, worries you terribly. So you asked him. But he wasn't lying when he said it wasn't him. I mean, it was him who stole your credits. But not the smoke. He's forest born and bred. He'd never do a thing like that."

"That's what he said," murmured Belmarsh. "How did you-"

"Like I said. I see through the fear to the truth.

Apparently." Andrea could still hear the river; it calmed her, guided her intuition.

"He's been hanging out with a bad crowd from another village. I saw one day, when we were out foraging. He picked up certain leaves-"

"Forbidden leaves."

"They're reserved for adults because of the effect they can have if consumed in certain ways."

"Basically, you thought your son was a drug dealer."

"Yes." Belmarsh stared down at the ground far beneath them. Andrea kept her eyes fixed very firmly on him.

"He isn't. He didn't start a fire making happy-ash to sell to Uffingdale, and he didn't steal your credits to buy equipment. He stole your credits because he wants to go to Sheffield and find his mother. You told him she went there to work. You didn't mention she'd gone there to make a new life with someone else."

"You can stop now."

"You were afraid of the scandal. But the Elders found out anyway."

"I said-"

"She didn't respect the laws of the forest, or you, or the promises she-"

"Please! Please, I know! Stop!"

Andrea snapped her mouth shut. He was crying. Two big fat tears, one rolling down each cheek. He sniffed loudly.

The river was quiet.

"I'm so sorry," said Andrea. "I overstepped. This is all a bit... New."

"I need to go and find my son," Belmarsh said, in a very small voice.

"Oh, yes. Yes, of course. I'll, um, go down first so you can... Yes."

She edged over to the ladder and descended as fast as she dared while still retaining a shred of dignity. Belmarsh followed, swift and nimble despite his age. She stepped back so he could pass, but he paused. "Tell Berta I still miss her, sometimes," he said. "And her apprentice needs a little work on her bedside manner, but otherwise shows great promise. Thank you, dear."

She watched him walk away, towards the dwelling trees, and took a deep breath. Then she made her way back to the Elders' Cabin, where the Eldermost was waiting for her.

"He is leaving the council, I take it?" said the Eldermost, ushering her inside. They sat together at the Elders' table, just the two of them.

"I think it's for the right reasons. He needs time with his son, and the council needs time to heal, don't you think?"

"More than you know," said the Eldermost. "And you will help us?"

Andrea smiled. "If I can."

The Eldermost poured water into two cups, and handed one to Andrea.

"The vine must find its own route to climb." He raised his cup. "To the wisdom of the forest, and the truth of the river who feeds her."

"To the forest, and the river," said Andrea.

"So tell me," Berta said, directing her words at the trees around her. "How long have you lived in that cave down there?"

There was a pause, and then a wee voice said, "Since breakfast."

"I see. And how long do you intend to remain there?"

There was a scuffing noise, like someone kicking their heel into gravel. "F'rever."

"Really? Well, that's a very long time."

Silence

"I can tell you're an intrepid explorer. What supplies do you have with you?"

"Enough for one. Not for two."

"Ah, don't worry on my account, boy. I'm not at all intrepid. I like my comforts. Hot meals, blankets, bed time stories. That kind of thing. Does your mother tell you bedtime stories?"

Another pause and then, "Yes."

"Does she, now? Well, you'll be missing that tonight when it's all dark down there and you're all alone. I'll be sure to think of you, from under my blankets and all. Did you bring any blankets?"

"I've got everything I need."

"Of course."

Berta picked up a shard of limestone from the mouth of the cave. It broke off at the edges when she rubbed it with her thumb, like a crumbly cheese.

"Have you got a blanket with you?" said the boy. She'd put his age at no more than eight, but he spoke clearly and with absolute conviction, despite the waves of anxiety rolling off him.

"Not with me, boy, no. Is that your name, boy?"

"Of course not. Nobody's called Boy."

"Oh. So what is your name?"

"Neil."

"Right, Neil. No, sorry, Neil, I don't have a blanket. There's a village nearby though. There might be one there. It's called Neverhulme, do you know it?"

"Could you go and get me one, then?"

"Now then, Neil, you seem like a bright boy. What do you think I'm going to say to that?"

"All in all, I would say... No. I think you're going to say no."

"Told you you're a bright boy. I bet you know

what's going to happen next."

"I'm not coming out."

"Just when things were going so well."

"I'm not. Ever. I live here, now."

"Without any blankets. Or food."

"I can fish!"

"You'll be a long time waiting, Neil. That spring down there's brand new. It won't grow you fish for a long time. Not 'til it comes out into the light and joins the river. That's quite a ways from here."

"You're lying."

"Do you see any fish?"

There was a pause, then a splashing sound, and finally an unhappy little cough.

"How about this, Neil. You come out and have a chat with me, and then you can go back in there if you want. I've got some sandwiches you can have. Might tide you over for a bit until you work out which lichen are poisonous and which you can safely lick off the rocks to survive. What d'you say?"

There was a bit of angry splashing, a cough or two - nervous habit, sounded like - and then a slap, slap, slap of feet on wet rock before two little brown hands reached out to grip the rim of the hole. Berta didn't help him; she just waited until he'd pulled himself out and scrambled to his feet. He stood there, blinking up at the forest canopy, squinting as light streamed through. He was younger than she'd thought, or perhaps just smaller. Berta had always found it tricky to know where to place individual children on the path between squalling infant and young adult.

She opened up her packet of sandwiches, and offered them to him. He took one, with a polite 'thank you', and folded up his legs to sit cross-legged in front of her. He ate the sandwich in little bites, nibbling around the edges in a spiral. He was diligent at it, careful.

"'S nice," he said, when he'd finished the first one. "Is that plums?"

"Plum jam. Made it myself. It goes very well with the cheese, don't you think?"

He nodded. "Cheese doesn't go in sandwiches with plums, normally."

"Thank you for noticing. That's my adventure, you see. Sandwich fillings. Would you care for another?"

"Yes, please."

They shared Berta's lunch in a companionable silence, then sat there together. Berta poured tea from her vacuum flask to drink, while Neil sipped at water from a bottle he produced from the tiny rucksack he wore on his back.

"I was thinking," Neil said. "Now I live in the cave, perhaps you could bring me sandwiches every day? I mean, I'd swap. I could find you pretty stones. There's a lot of pretty stones in there."

Berta gave him a long look. Enough was enough. He was a sturdy, well-fed boy, with hair neatly cut and bound into a pony tail at the nape of his neck. He wore no more than a morning's dirt on his skin.

"I don't think you belong out here, do you, Neil? Not to live."

He stuck out his plump, wet lower lip. But beyond the defiance there was something else. His shoulders were - not shaking, exactly, more vibrating. With a thousand little hurts and worries. He was just as anxious now as he'd been in the cave.

"Neil, look at Berta. Look in my eyes."

He obeyed her without thinking. His eyes were big and brown, and the truth lay just behind them, barely hidden. Berta let the river rush through, and Knew.

"Your eyes are amazing," said Neil, staring at her

slack-jawed. "There's these bits of kind of like gold in them."

"I have no idea what you're talking about. Now, then. What's all this about your silly old mother stopping you climbing trees?"

"She hates me," said Neil.

"No, my dear." Berta got to her feet, and reached out for his hand. "Trust me. She doesn't. I'd know."

Neil took Berta's hand, and let her lead him back through the forest.

Andrea sat in the story circle with Orchid. He was wearing woollen leggings striped in brown and green, and a bright scarlet sweater that was a little big for his slender shoulders. His dark hair was scraped back in a neat bun, showing off his sharp cheekbones and almond eyes. He juggled with pine cones, and pointed out the tree-house where he lived with his parents and their lovers and his siblings and half-siblings. He talked about how much he loved coming back to the forest after a season of wandering from village to village with the troupe.

"It's like coming back from a two-dimensional world," he said. "Here life is in three dimensions. We have breadth, width and height." He glanced up towards the top of the tree in the middle of the story circle. "The canopy protects us, and gives us homes. The plants beneath feed us fruit. Below that are the vegetables and herbs, the medicines and dyes. We have all we need here. To me, White Water is chaos. Like a house with the roof blown off."

Andrea smiled. "But we have the river."

"And that is how we are, in Yorkshire," he replied. "We each have a little of the whole. We are like the forest. All growing together towards the sun."

Andrea let Orchid's voice wash over her,

soothing her. She was startled by Berta's voice booming across the clearing.

"Is that there the boy your Matt's sweet on?"

Orchid looked up with a little frown of confusion.

"Take no notice," Andrea said. "She's overexcited and probably very much looking forward to gloating."

"Are you done, Andrea?" Berta said. She was holding the hand of a young boy. He had a backpack on his back and tear stains on his grubby face.

"I see you found Neil," said Orchid.

"Indeed I did," said Berta. "Where do his family live?"

Orchid pointed at the complex of trees in front of them, a jumble of tree-houses connected by rustic wooden walkways, some at dizzying heights. "Third back, five along, fifth tier."

"Right," said Berta. "Go and fetch them, would you? And you." She pointed at Andrea. "Get the elders. We need to tell them about this smoke they're so worried about."

Berta walked back through the forest with Andrea at her side. The day was moving on, and the sunshine had a thickness about it, like old whisky.

"I had no idea trees did that," said Andrea.

"Trees do a great many things," Berta replied. "Never underestimate a tree. Releasing clouds of pollen that look like smoke are the tip of the iceberg, believe me."

"Still, you'd think the Elders would know about it."

"I think today the Elders have learned that when one person says they saw 'smoke' they should consider whether or not they are a reliable witness. If it was someone from the village, fair enough. If it's a journalist who normally lives in Sheffield they really should ask more questions."

"And then there's Neil."

"Hm."

"You were talking with his family for a long time."

"They have a child who believes if he doesn't climb every tree in the forest in a certain order, bad things will happen. And then he runs away to a hole under the ground when he's upset. I had a good deal to say to them. They have much work to do."

"Will you go back to help them?"

"Of course I will."

"Even though it's Neverhulme?"

There was a sneaky little grin at the corner of Andrea's mouth that Berta didn't quite like the look of. "I have no idea what you mean."

"No need to be tetchy."

"I'm not tetchy. I'm hungry. I gave most of my lunch to an eight-year old boy."

They paused by the bridge at the edge of the forest. Andrea rustled about in her bag for a moment, then produced something wrapped up in hemp.

"What's that?" asked Berta.

"It's for you."

Berta took the gift and raised it to her nose. She sniffed, sniffed again and then took in a long, deep breath. Her senses were alight with cinnamon and ginger and nutmeg. She stripped off the covering and opened up the box inside.

Spiced apple muffins. Goodness.

"Thank you," Berta said. She offered one to Andrea, took one for herself, and put the lid back on the rest. They sat on the old bench by the bridge, and Berta took the time to enjoy every single bite.

"I'm proud of you, girl," said Berta.

"Because I gave you cake?"

"Because you passed the test."

"I did?"

"Of course. The Eldermost is very impressed. You have your first client! And you gave old Belmarsh a kick up the arse while you were at it. Long overdue, that."

"Oh." She looked all pink and pleased. "I thought I'd failed. I mean, I didn't find out a thing about the smoke."

That's accountancy for you. So literal. "Therein lies the lesson, my girl. We don't find out what we want to know. We find out what's in front of us."

She watched Andrea soak up that truth like a sponge, then held out the box of muffins. "More cake, dear?"

"Thanks," said Andrea, with a smile that brought out her dimples.

They crossed the river back to White Water and, for now, left Neverhulme in the care of the trees.

Woodless
by LH Annable

There was only one path through the forest. The trick to getting through the trees was to ignore anything they said and to move fast. If she slowed down to listen, they noticed her human warmth and scent, and they would start to unwind their limbs and crack open their trunks, ready to eat.

But they said fascinating things, words she'd never heard before, and so sometimes she lingered. Trini did too, listening as intently as he could and staying right until the moment a tree's maw opened and its black gullet became visible. Then he'd run, laughing and shouting out the words he'd learned.

Mala stood at the edge of the meadow, near the beginning of the path, digging her bare toes tight into the earth as if she could plant herself here and not have to step forward. She'd skirted the edge of the forest for a mile, a small useless flint knife clutched in her fist. Her palm was hot with sweat. Her uncle's field ran down almost to the edge of the trees, and she'd taken care not to crush even a single tight green head of the early wheat. She shivered and yanked her woollen cloak back up around her shoulders. It was still too big for her. Her mother had been a tall woman.

The edge of the forest was fringed with fruit and nut trees. Apples, pears, hazelnuts and plums were tangled together as if locked in a fight. Of course, no one could eat their fruits.

Aunt Lita had shown them what an apple could do, once. She'd cut it open with one flick of her flint and the seeds inside had twitched and then writhed out of the flesh like grubs, burrowing down into Aunt Lita's palm hard and quick enough to draw blood, and Mala and her brother had jumped back, gasping.

"Never, ever trust a tree," Aunt Lita had warned, then she'd dug them out with the tip of her flint. She threw the seeds down and crushed them with the butt of her blade. There had been a faint high shriek as the seeds popped. She thrust her rough, dirt-stained palm in their faces. "Never."

It wasn't the only time Mala had known a tree draw blood. She stepped closer and the trees began to rustle, even though there was no breeze. She clutched her knife tighter, and forced herself to step past the ancient and twisted apple tree that stood guard. Trini was in here, somewhere. He might already be eaten. She walked forward, misery rising with every step.

"Human," the apple tree said, and she flinched. Its voice was low and hollow, the sounds mushy and indistinct, like Lita and Gall after half a bottle of moonshine. It dropped a perfect green apple in her path.

Mala shrank from it and edged past, gaze glued to its smooth skin in case the seeds broke free.

"Human," it said again, and began creaking out words she didn't understand. "Listen. High density concrete. Low alloy steel. Platinum. Neodymium."

She hurried along the path, and the voice of the apple faded. The trees stretched off all around her, limbs thin and starved and beginning to twitch. Then the trees began to speak.

The old lore said that trees had once been friendly. They'd covered the earth and hadn't eaten anyone at all. They had lived and died alongside people in peace. What must it have been like to be alive then? She tried to imagine winters eased with wood fires, and couldn't.

But then poison had come from the stars and the world had changed.

"Antibiotics," a tall skinny pine tree wheezed from a slit low down on its trunk. "Tetracyclines. Opiates. Vasodilators."

The words didn't mean anything to her. They didn't mean anything to anyone, though the bard said that they had done before the poison had come. The bard had unfurled a long strip of dried skin on which she'd written a list of tree-speech. Gall had forbidden the bard from reciting them.

"Leave me alone," Mala said and hurried on.

Here and there the path forked off into much smaller tracks, likely made by hogs and foxes, but she ignored those. She guessed where Trini had gone.

She moved at a light trot, a pace she knew she could keep up all day. As she went further in, the morning faded to a green twilight gloom. Words echoed around her, high and low, some loud, some quiet, as if the trees might be different in the way that people were different. Were they? They were all born from a single tree, the bard said, all connected.

Trini would tell her that she should ask them and find out. Misery bore down on her in a thousand whispers that burrowed into her thoughts as surely as the apple seeds had wormed into Lita's palm.

"Woven polyesters, acrylonitrile butadiene styrene."

"Shut up," she said, finally. "Shut up! If you want to talk so much, tell me where Trini is."

"Human. Listen," an oak said in a low grating rumble. "Hydrogen. Petrol. Uranium."

She sped up, and so did her heart. She'd lost track of time, she realised. Her legs felt like she'd been walking all morning but it couldn't be more than five miles. It would take another ten to reach the North Road and freedom, but she was sure she'd find Trini sooner than that. She was nearing The Place, and she wished with everything inside her that Trini hadn't been such an idiot and that they could be back in the yurt listening to the bard's stories, eating dried hog and small green early onions.

The path widened gradually, and she saw a scrap of wool caught on the thorns of a bramble. She plucked it off. This was from Trini's cloak, a ragged hand-me-down from Uncle Gall, and it had a smear of blood on it. A branch reached down and slapped the knife from her hand, and began to wind around her wrist. She wrenched her arm away.

"Trini," she called, starting to run. "Trini." Around her, branches flexed with sharp cracks but she dodged them when they reached for her. She stumbled into a wide clearing, a place where she had hoped never to be again. The trees fell silent.

"No," she moaned, when she saw his body at the foot of the vast oak that grew in the middle of the clearing. She ran to him. "Trini? Oh no." He'd taken Gall's machete for protection. The tree had a foot long gouge across its maw, and a pale raw scar where the bark had been torn away. Trini's chest and stomach were mangled and bloodied and his nails were broken where he'd clawed at the tree, but his eyes were open and he smiled at her.

"It's all buried in the earth," he said, grinning up at her. "What we used to be before the poison. It told me, when I was inside. Mala, it's wonderful! Their roots go down to the old cities."

"How is that wonderful?" She pushed his hair back from his forehead as the blood drained from her face. She'd never be able to get him back to the farm. "Forget that. It's not important," she said. "Can you walk?"

"No."

"Trini." She began to cry. "Why did you come here?"

Trini blinked up at her and grimaced. "She died here. I had to come back, Mala. I had to know why. I wanted to talk to the tree that killed her. It remembers her. I think they remember everything." He sounded awestruck.

"Humans," the tree said. It was vast and twisted and its arms were as big as the trunk of the smaller trees. One of them snaked down and wound itself tight around her ankle. "Listen."

"Why should I?" Mala screamed, and snatched the machete up. "You don't listen to us!" The blade stuck deep in the branch and she panted in terror as another one slowly unfurled and crept towards her. She yanked her blade free and hacked again. "Why?" she screamed again. "Why do you always ask us to listen?"

The tree began to slowly winch her closer, and then stopped, as if considering. Had anyone ever asked it a question? "Because you cannot help but obey," it said, after a while, as if it had had to search for words that meant anything. "You are," and it stopped, as if thinking. "Curious." It inched her closer and its wounded maw began to open. The smell of raw wood filled the air.

"You want to learn. Your curiosity will kill you." It shivered, as if pleased with its thought. "It always has. It always will. We know your history and we can guess your future. We read the bones of your ancient constructions with our roots."

The strength in its limb was terrifying. Mala yanked at it but it was like trying to move solid stone. "Don't you care about anything?" Mala asked. "About us?"

"Your burned us in our millions," the tree said.

"Why should we care about humans?"

Mala blinked. No one burned wood. No one used wood for anything. Last summer the lightning storms had set fire to a whole forest on the other side of the valley. Everyone in the surrounding encampments had died from the poison in the air. More fool them, Gall had said, for lingering there in the summer. The bard called the poison a self defence mechanism, like the tusks on the hogs. "I-I didn't know. But that was so long ago. Don't punish us!"

"It is not punishment," the tree said, slowly. "It is farming. You should understand that well enough, human."

Mala clawed at the dried oak leaves on the ground. The earth was soft and she moaned in terror as her fingers slid through it. Had her mother died this same way, as helpless as a minnow against the stabbing beak of a fisherbird? She dug her heels in and pulled against its grip as hard as she could; then behind her she heard a groan.

Trini loomed above her with the machete. He was swaying, and blood ran thickly from the bite on his stomach. "Run when you can," he said, slurring, then raised his arms and brought the machete down with a broken cry, then once more.

The branches splintered and cracked, and she yanked her limbs free and scrambled to her feet.

"Run, Mala," Trini said, and caught her hand and squeezed it. "Run. Please."

"Listen, human," the tree said and Mala thought she heard a low hateful satisfaction in the sound.

Trini raised his arms in front of the tree, head back, laughing. "I'm listening."

She ran.

Petr, Husband of Fevronia
by Ekaterina Fawl

The heart of the forest, Marfa had said: through black brush and dead trees into the quiet place where the birds wouldn't sing, the air wouldn't move. She went there herself, years ago, to ask the forest witch for a child.

Another time Petr would have berated her: dealing with witches was a grave sin. Now, worn down by pain and fever, he hadn't the strength to be righteous.

"But that didn't work," he only said. Marfa had been married to his brother for a decade now. They'd all given up hope.

"The price was too much. You have to ask, at least."

He left his horse at the edge of the forest and went on foot, and soon couldn't find a path. He crashed through dry undergrowth, and thin branches whipped his face bloody and ripped his boils open. On each step a pulling ache flared through his insides, deep and shameful.

He stumbled over nothing; the pain of the fall stunned him. He lay still, too weak even to scream, and his broken skin leaked pus into the wet moss.

There was a soft sound in the perfect silence. He opened his eyes, almost hoping for a wolf, for a quicker end.

A hare stared at him sideways with an eye dark and round like a ripe plum. It caught Petr's glance and flexed its shoulders, ready to bolt.

"I won't hurt you. Couldn't harm a fly right now."

The hare sank down on its haunches, taking Petr at his word.

"The witch," Petr told the hare. Sickness churned his mind, and this seemed like the thing to do. "Fevronia. Where is she?"

The hare turned and jumped through the branches in a long graceful arc.

Petr crawled after it, dragging himself on his elbows. For a while he thought he saw a twitching tail through the mess of undergrowth. When he lost sight of it he kept going without direction, muttering jumbled prayers.

The forest shrank back a little, and he was in a clearing. In the middle of it, quiet and pale as the birches around her, stood a young woman: barefoot and bareheaded, with only a short shift to cover her.

He pushed to his knees and drew his sword.

"You're under my protection," he told her. A half-naked girl, alone in the woods - he didn't need to ask what had happened. "Are they still around? I'll fight them off, I'll take you home. You won't be hurt again, I promise."

Her eyes were very bright, the hungry green shade of spring grass. The hare hopped around her feet, nosed at her ankles. She wasn't scared, or hurt, or lost. She was home.

"Fevronia?"

She tilted her head to a side, as a bird would.

"Help me," he begged. The boils on his face were huge now, pulsing. He felt them shift as he spoke.

She touched his cheek. Her fingers were cold like river pebbles and his pain trickled between them, melted away.

"Serpent's blood," she said. "What happened?"

He hid his face against her hand and told her everything.

It all started a week ago.

"That thing in my room is not my husband," Marfa had said.

"What's he done now?" Petr asked.

It wasn't the first time. He'd played the peacemaker for them ever since Marfa had married Pavel, since Petr himself was small enough for her to cuddle and kiss him and call him her handsome prince. He'd cling to her then, melt against her breasts and belly and there had been nothing wrong with that.

They'd not done that for years now, but he still remembered the warmth and the soft give of her flesh. He shouldn't even be standing this close to her, he knew that.

"No, it's not your brother! It's not our knjaz! Pavel's gone, it's not him!"

She clutched at his arm so hard he worried she'd score her hand bloody on the rings of his mail. She caught him on his way from the training field. He was still fully clad and grateful for that, as if armour could shield him from any weakness within. He'd never seen her like this. She'd been angry with Pavel plenty, but never scared.

"What is it, then?"

"The Enemy." She shuddered, and her eyes welled up. "Do you believe me?"

He knew what she meant. There was only one enemy to the human race: the Trickster, the Deceiver, and Marfa wouldn't utter his name even in a whisper.

"Well... If it is... Shouldn't we tell the priests?"

"I can't. The whole town will know, and I can't. Petr, it came here for me. It stole Pavel's face to - it wants me, it's relentless..."

"You didn't," he started, and couldn't say a crass word to her. "You wouldn't, not with..."

"It's the Enemy. The Seducer. Petr, brother, kinsman, help me."

He followed her to her rooms, gripping his sword, praying silently. He didn't think he'd see the Devil in his own palace, but she was crying and he had to help.

Pavel was in bed, bare-legged, languid. Petr had never seen his brother like that. He lingered by the door, about to bow and apologise.

"Kill it," said Marfa. "Petr, I beg you, kill it!"

"Ah," Pavel said. "Finally decided it's time for a younger husband? You know, Petr, she's been eyeing you for years, just waiting for you to grow up so she could ride a fresh stallion. Oh, don't blush, little brother. You've dreamt about this since I married her. You think I don't see how you stare at her tits, how you sniff after her?"

It was his face, his voice, but the words were unthinkable. Pavel would never say that. It was all a lie. Petr had never - he had crushed every such thought, spent hours in relentless prayer every time he'd slipped up.

"Did she give you a taste? Or will that be your reward for killing your kin? Did she tell you it's my fault she's barren? Did she promise you'll fill her belly, give the land an heir?"

"Kill it!" Marfa screamed. "Don't listen, it's poison!"

"It's not even about her, much as you'd love to get between her legs." Pavel slid off the bed and stepped closer. "It's my throne you want. You ache to be the knjaz."

There was nothing in his eyes that Petr could recognise, nothing human at all.

"She must've convinced you it's for the greater good," Pavel said. "You're a gutless little snake, you need to feel righteous before you take what you want. What did she tell you, my pious Petr? That I'm the Devil?"

He laughed, and Petr drew his sword and slashed deep, for a quick, sure kill.

A spray of blood hit his face, every drop scalding hot. For one moment he couldn't breathe - and then the body fell and spasmed at his feet, and he screamed with horror and joy.

It wasn't a human body. It was enormous, long, scaly, with a wide maw and clawed paws. The blood spurting from the wound was thick, black as tar.

"What's going on?" said Pavel's voice.

His brother was in the room, just behind him, familiar and worried. Petr turned to point at the monster's twitching carcass.

It was gone. There was no black blood on the carpet, none on Petr. The sword in his hand was gleaming, unmarred.

"Husband!" Marfa threw herself at Pavel and covered his face with kisses. "Where have you been?"

"Hunting," said Pavel slowly, as if unsure. "Did I not say?"

Petr went straight to his room and lay in bed until morning, sleepless.

He still felt every drop of the serpent's blood on his skin. It itched and burned, worse by the minute. He scratched himself until his fingers came away bloody. Then he wrapped his hands in the sheets and writhed on his bed in agony, hoping the pain would stop.

By dawn he was covered in seeping sores and boils. By the end of the week every healer in Murom had given up on him, and the priests were hurrying him to take the last rites. And he would have, but he dreaded the confession.

When he'd drawn his sword - he couldn't swear before God if right then, in that moment, he had truly believed he was striking down the Enemy.

This sickness, this curse had to be the proof of his sin and his just punishment. He felt death circling him and he couldn't rest, couldn't pray, couldn't find the courage to give in. And then Marfa told him there was one more thing they could try.

Fevronia listened silently, didn't hurry him when he choked up, didn't flinch once. He still knelt at her feet, and the last of his strength was fading. Little by little he leaned all his weight against her palm and she held him upright, strong as a man, as earth itself.

"Can you stop this? Can you save me?"

"There's a price."

"Anything. I'm rich. Gold, furs, jewels - just name what you want."

"I want you."

He pulled back and slumped down to sit on his heels. She still held her hand out, waiting for his answer. Waiting for him to place his hand in hers.

"You want to... wed me?"

Her beautiful eyes were hollow, intent, the eyes of a wolf in winter. He was right, that was what she wanted - all of him, forever. He ducked his head to hide his face, and then didn't know where to look. Her shift barely covered the soft swell of her thighs. Her bare knees were smooth and round like apples, and her small toes were spread in the moss, pink and delicate. Lust clawed through his fevered body, a new kind of pain.

"I can't. My brother is the knjaz of Murom. I have to marry a boyar's daughter."

"I can't force you," she said and stepped away.

"No, wait - ask anything else - I'm dying, have pity!"

"If you won't be mine, why should I care if you live or die?"

He clutched at the dry grass, too weak to even stand up. He wouldn't make it back home. He'd die in the forest, without rites and burial. Beasts would eat his flesh and gnaw on his bones, and his soul would be damned. The last thing he did would have been bargaining with a witch. If he lived he could repent, atone...

"I'll do it," he said.

She handed him a burdock leaf with a clump of green mud in it. It smelled of swamp water and braga gone sour.

"Put this on all your sores. Leave one for the sickness to drain out."

And then she was gone, as if she'd melted in the gaps between the birch trees. He pulled off his clothes, wet with pus and blood, and smeared cold salve on his skin wherever he could reach. He was still writhing on the ground, trying to slap some on the pustules on his back, when his arms turned leaden and the world went dark.

He woke past dawn, and at first wondered why he hadn't heard the roosters' call. The salve had dried and flaked off his skin and there were no marks left, no lingering redness. On his chest, at the spot he'd left uncovered, there was a small dry scab: a clean shallow wound healing fast.

Fevronia wasn't around. He thought to call out for her, but instead grabbed his clothes and fled. He ran a mile before he tired. He was cured.

"It's the Lord's miracle," said the priests. Their eyes were narrowed, suspicious. Somehow they knew.

Marfa told everyone she'd sent him on a pilgrimage around local churches. Petr nodded along to her story and let his brother hug him and cry with joy, and throw a feast in his honour. He waited until they were alone and Pavel seemed well plied with wine.

"I found myself a wife," he said then.

"Oh, good," said Pavel. "I thought you'd never look up from your Bible to notice a woman. Who is she, who's her father?"

"Nobody. She's..."

"A peasant?"

"She's very wise, very skillful," Petr said quickly. "And so beautiful. She has the fairest skin, and her hair is like fine flax..."

"Petr, stop."

"I... I promised her."

"Well, you shouldn't have."

Petr nodded. His face was burning, as if the fever had come back.

"You're the next knjaz, Petr. Your life isn't your own, you belong to Murom. When I'm gone the boyars will look to usurp you. You have to marry well, to bind a strong family to you."

"I know."

"Is there a bastard on the way?"

"No."

"Thank the Lord for that, at least. Send her a rich gift. Take what you want from the treasury, be generous. Apologise and forget her."

"I'm sorry."

"Don't apologise to me. I should've had you married by now - I keep thinking you're still a boy. We'll do it this autumn, Marfa and I will find you the best bride..."

Petr listened silently and worried the scab on his chest. It itched, and soon bled through his shirt, and he couldn't stop poking at it.

He kept scratching at his chest all night long, as if he could get his fingers under his breastbone and rip out the ache that spread there. His skin was swelling, heating up all over, rising in welts.

It went a lot faster that time. When the first pustules burst under his fingers he laughed, and couldn't stop even when healers and priests crowded his bed again.

"Stupid boy," said Marfa when he'd sent everyone else away and they were alone. "You didn't pay her, did you?"

"She wanted me! I promised - why would she want me? She has power over life and death. What's one little princeling to her, what's all Murom's riches to someone like that?"

"Even a witch is still a woman."

"But she only saw me like this." He clawed at his monstrously swollen face, digging his fingernails into the sores. Marfa pushed his hands down; he tried to fight her, thoughtless and angry, but she was stronger than him now.

"You have to go back," she said. "I'll teach you what to tell her."

He barely heard what she said next. She was right. He had to go back.

He couldn't find the clearing. When he could no longer walk or crawl he lay on the ground and called out her name. She wouldn't hear, he could barely manage a whisper, but he kept calling.

Suddenly she was there, crouched above him. Her beautiful green eyes were bloodshot: she'd been crying, like a girl, like a jilted bride.

"Why should I care if you live or die?" she yelled in his face. "Why should I care?"

"I'm dying," he told her. "I'm lost to Murom, Pavel has to name a new heir. My soul is damned thrice over. I betrayed my brother, my God, and you. But, what's left of me, if there's anything - that's yours."

He'd already reneged on their bargain, and these were empty words. He wanted to die away from the kingdom he'd lost, away from judgement and pity, next to the one who knew all his worst secrets, next to the woman who wanted him.

He covered her cold toes with his palm and stilled, ready to let the sickness run its course. She was crying again and her wails were a lullaby, softly pulling him into the dark.

When he opened his eyes again he was naked, and his skin was clear. His whole body sang with strength, itching to move.

Fevronia sat by a tree trunk a few steps away, with her shift pulled tightly over her knees. She glared at him and wiped her eyes and nose.

"Just leave," she said. "There's no price, it's a gift. You can go."

He tried to recall Marfa's lesson; she'd put something in his pocket to give to the witch. He rifled through his clothes and found a handful of flax, and stood up, unashamed to be bare before her.

"I'll marry you," he said, making it a solemn vow. "If, from this, you make me a shirt and a pillow."

He looked at the small clump in his hand and only then understood: this wasn't a promise. It was a rebuke, a new insult. Marfa hadn't taught him how to make things right, only how to trick the witch and get out of his bargain.

"Wait, that's not--" he stammered, but Fevronia smiled and got up. There was a tree branch in her hand, a stump half foot long.

"I'll make you a shirt to cover you," she said. "And a pillow for you to rest on, and sheets for your bed, and cloth for your table. If, from this, you make me a loom."

It jutted from her small fist obscenely, her fingers barely closing over the thick wood. Petr stared at the pad of her thumb, pressed against a knot in the bark, and his own flesh stiffened, as if it felt her touch. The tangled clump of flax he held was the same colour the hair between her legs would be, and it would feel just like this under his fingers.

This had to be a heathen ritual, an old dark sorcery. They said the words and brought the offerings and now the magic was loose and he was helpless, bound to the single path like a flying arrow, like a falling stone.

He reached for her, wordlessly, as if in a dream, and she fell into his arms, and the scent of her skin made him weak with want.

"Not yet," he managed when she pulled his hands onto her body. "First we must wed before God."

She grunted with impatient need and her eyes blazed silver.

He stared into that horrible, harsh glow, and heard a sound like a thousand rolls of thunder, deafening, painful. The air hummed and quivered around them, as if stirred by monstrous wings, as if the forest was on fire. There was a sigh, an intake of breath, a half-sound that was almost a silence. Somehow Petr knew: if that voice spoke a word it would rend flesh from their bones. He had to halt this spell and save them both.

He cupped his hand over Fevronia's eyes.

"Stop," he pleaded, and she did. The light blinked out under his palm and whatever witchcraft she had woven was broken for the moment. He wanted to tell her she didn't need threats and magic, that he wouldn't deceive her, she only had to wait a little longer. But she'd be a fool to believe him again.

He kissed her. Her breath tasted of new snow and autumn berries; she kissed him back, and soon he didn't know how to stop. It was witchcraft, he knew that, but by the time their bodies locked together on the bed of grass and rotting leaves he saw nothing wrong with that.

When all his strength was spent she still held him, stroked his face and played with his hair. Her smile was like sunlight on water, bright and sweet.

"Are we wed?" she asked.

"We'll have the ceremony."

By the time they rode into Murom Pavel was ready to bless their marriage. That, of course, was Marfa's doing. The boyars didn't dare argue openly - the bishop was the only one to say anything.

"Do you understand what blasphemy this is?" he whispered to Petr on their way to the church.

"She's just a peasant."

"I know what she is. Do you know what will happen when I bless her? When I tell her to kiss the Holy Cross? Do you want everyone to see that?"

Petr didn't know. He imagined Fevronia's fair skin burning under the touch of the holy relics, like his own had been scalded by the serpent's blood, and he faltered when they stood together in the church's doorway.

"Is this safe for you?" he asked.

"Petr, it's only a ceremony," she said and calmly led him to the altar.

Nothing went wrong: they didn't misstep or misspeak, the candles didn't go out. Nothing went wrong for days and weeks after that, though he wouldn't have noticed. He and Fevronia had barely left their rooms. He felt like every need of his body and soul could be sated by the taste of her skin, everything worth knowing could be learnt from the lines of her face and the shade of her eyes.

Then a few boyars cornered him on his way to a feast.

"She's bewitched you, and she'll curse all of Murom," they said. "Did you see - at every meal she gathers crumbs from our table."

"She was a peasant. She grew up poor, every crumb counted."

"It's for curses! That food touched our lips, she can hex whoever was eating it! She curses the crumbs and feeds them to her cat--"

"That's not a cat," Petr said. Fevronia's hare sat by the door, listening.

"Of course it isn't! It's a familiar of the Devil!"

"You're fools," he said. Marriage had made him bold, smug. "But, fine. If I see her do that I'll talk to her."

That day at supper as the cups were refilled the second time Fevronia shook back the sleeve of her dress, reached her bare arm across the table and began plucking at the scraps scattered between the dishes. Half-chewed gristle someone had spat out, bread crust soaked in goose fat, a slimy core of a baked apple. She grabbed all that and held in her fist, and everyone stared.

It was strange, and a little disgusting. If Petr saw someone else's wife doing that at the knjaz's table he'd be offended too.

"Fevronia," he said.

She opened her hand. Familiar heady scent filled the room. In the dead silence the bishop gasped softly.

Fevronia's palm was clean, and in it lay three big chunks of myrrh.

Afterwards they had their first proper spat.

"What were you thinking?" he yelled, pacing their bedroom.

"But they love myrrh, it's holy!"

"What are we to you, Fevronia? How stupid do you think we are? I knew you were mocking them, their fears, our faith, and they know it too!"

"It's not my fault they're ripe for mocking."

"They're my people! You wanted to be with me. Well, you're in my house now, and you have to live by its rules."

"I don't have to be with you here," she said, and her eyes were hollow and mean again. He's not seen that since he'd first kissed her.

"What would you do? Take me to your forest, magic up a hut to keep me in? Or turn me into a wolf for the winter, so I can fend for myself? Or make me into a tree whenever you're not in the mood to use me? I've been wondering what this is," he pointed at the animal on the floor. "Is it your last husband?"

"Petr, it's a hare."

The hare gave him a dismayed look, left a clump of droppings on the rug and scampered away. Petr stared after it, ashamed of his anger.

"Come here," she said and he knelt at her feet and embraced her, and nothing seemed worth arguing about.

"Don't goad them," he asked anyway. "I know it must irk how they think of you. But if you really were a peasant they'd be worse."

"It doesn't matter much. As long as Pavel is knjaz nobody will bother us."

When the hunting party brought Pavel's gored body home Petr couldn't look at it. He had to find out what had happened, which servant had let his brother come to harm, where his boyars were when the boar had charged. He tried questioning them but hadn't lasted long before he fled to his rooms to find solace in Fevronia's arms.

There was a slaughtered goat by their bed, its black legs still bound. Fevronia - barefoot, bareheaded - was draining the last of its blood into a clay pot. Marfa was with her, arranging small candles on the floor in a circle.

"We'll bring him back," Fevronia said. "The price is high, but between the three of us we can bear it."

"No," he muttered, horrified.

"Petr, I need him," Marfa said. Her voice was a raspy whisper, wrecked from crying.

"You love him," he said. "Would you rip his soul out of Heaven?"

"We all need him!" shouted Fevronia. "Without him you'll have to be their knjaz, and you're not theirs, you're mine!"

"This is madness. We're not going to raise the dead. I won't let you damn yourselves, and I won't let you do that to Pavel."

Marfa sobbed, nodded and threw the candles down.

"I can't force you." Fevronia stood up and easily shouldered the dead goat. It would be startling if he hadn't already known how strong she was.

"I'll take this to the kitchens," she said and left.

She didn't show up for the vigil, or the funeral, or the wake. She returned at dawn and crawled into bed with him naked, still reeking of blood. She clung to him and he held her and loved her, frenzied, trying to chase away the thought of his brother in a wooden box, under heavy dirt.

In the morning there should have been his coronation, but the boyars called the council instead.

"I won't bless you to reign until she's gone," the bishop said. "We want her out of the palace and out of Murom."

"She's my wife," Petr said. Fevronia had seen this coming, this was what she had feared. "She's just..."

"Even if she was just a peasant," said someone else. "All our wives are nobles. You're not going to put her above them."

Fevronia sat by his side, pale and beautiful, regal in her jewelled dress. She didn't say a word, didn't blink once.

The men kept talking, reasoning with him, making threats. Pavel's crown was on the table before them, and they wouldn't give it to him until he gave in.

The crown was his by right. He'd craved it all his life, even knowing his brother had to die for him to have it. It was made for their grandfather, had been in his family for almost a century...

Craftsmanship wasn't up to much back then: he'd just noticed that the spikes were uneven and some gems were missing at the rim.

"She must go, Petr," said Miroslav, Pavel's old friend. "We've decided to settle this honourably, give her treasure to take with her. We'll open all the coffers and let her choose whatever she wants."

Fevronia stood, ripped her high pearl collar off her neck and threw it at their feet. There were three rows of gem-inlaid bracelets on her wrists; she took each off and flung at them silently, and the boyars flinched in their seats, barely daring to duck.

"I want Petr," she said.

She shook off her headdress, wrenched emerald rings off her fingers. That was it - she'd cast off everything he'd given her, her shoes, her dress, and walk back to her forest in a linen shift, and he'd never see her again.

He stilled her hands before she could pull off her wedding ring.

"You're my wife. I go where you go," he said.

She stared at him; at first he thought she hadn't heard, didn't understand. Then her face flushed softly, like it did every time he kissed her. She took his hand and led him to the door.

"Bless your heart, boy," muttered Miroslav

behind them. Fevronia stopped and turned back, and two score men winced as one.

Only then did Petr understand what had just happened.

Fevronia wasn't casting off regal jewels to show how little she cared for Murom's riches. She didn't even care enough to do that. But the adornments were inlaid with silver and gold, and, as every child knew, metal hindered magic.

She'd never leave him. He was hers, he belonged to her by the terms of their bargain. She was going to fight for him. She'd been readying for battle, cladding herself in the armour of her kind: little more than her skin, her hair wild, bare toes spread and rooted.

He'd just saved forty lives, and he would keep it that way. Petr squeezed Fevronia's fingers and she didn't do anything, just left with him quietly.

He thought Fevronia would take him to the forest, but before they'd even left the palace they had a cadre of followers. His childhood friends and minor nobles wished to go with him into exile, to protect and support him. Perhaps they expected him to lead an insurrection. He was still too numb to argue or think that far ahead.

The men had supplies gathered and boats prepared, and Fevronia didn't seem to mind. They walked out of the city and let the river carry them where it would.

Everyone looked to him for orders. He told them he'd decide in the morning where they'd head and what they'd do. He spent the day lying in the boat with his head in Fevronia's lap, clutching at her hands.

"I'm glad we left," he told Fevronia when they stopped for the night.

"You're not," she said without sadness, like she'd say it would rain.

She looked glad. He never thought she'd been unhappy in the palace - he'd seen her smile, laugh, dance, seen her joyful at night and blissful in the morning. But he'd never seen her glow like this, be this content. The forest was her home, her kingdom. Of course she'd be happier here.

"I am glad," he insisted. "I thought I was destined for greatness. I thought I'd have a glorious reign, be a knjaz people would remember. But it's folly to guess at God's plan. Look."

He toed at the saplings they'd used to hang their pots over the fire.

"These would've been mighty oaks. They'd stand in this forest for a century and then wither and fall, and nobody would ever see or remember them. Instead we cut them down, and they gave us shelter and comfort. That's how it works out, always for the better."

She smiled, put her arms around him and pulled him into their tent.

That night was different, as if he was bewitched anew. They couldn't get enough of each other, both shaking with helpless tenderness, and the earth itself seemed to shift and quake beneath them.

In the morning that turned out to have been true. The ground under them was uneven and riddled with thick gnarled roots where none were before. The walls of their tent were pierced through with green branches that seem to have grown overnight, fast enough to rend oiled cloth.

Outside, where their fire had been, stood an oak three feet wide. Their pots and pans were scattered around it, pushed out by the trunk. The oak's crown spread over their whole camp and all the tents were askew - dislodged by roots, crowded by branches.

The men wandered around the tree, slapped its bark and laughed in stunned delight.

"Did you do that?" Petr asked, and Fevronia laughed and kissed him in full view of their small court.

He was still holding her when the messenger arrived.

"Knjaz," the man said. It was one of Pavel's captains, commander of his best hundred. "You have to come back."

The boyars had turned on each other, he said. None had a good enough claim to the throne and none would back down. The army had split, every faction backing a different man. The bishop had been murdered by Gleb's men for refusing to crown him - he said he'd rather die than give Murom to a villain. Gleb himself was killed by Miroslav's followers. The townspeople gathered on the streets, shouting that they wouldn't bow to usurpers and blasphemers.

Riders were spotted heading out north and west. All their neighbours would soon know, and their armies would clash at Murom's walls to decide which king would put his puppet on the empty throne. Someone had to unite the army, calm the people, defend the kingdom before it was too late, before there were puddles of blood on the streets, before their beautiful city was burning.

Murom was his, if he would claim it and save it. Petr looked at Fevronia's dear, fair face and couldn't ask her, couldn't even ask himself if she'd done that too.

He wasn't destined for greatness after all.

Murom welcomed him back, and the trouble in the palace was settled quickly. No foreign armies came for them - not then, not in all the years of his reign.

There were no wars, no plagues, no fires or floods, no famines, not even a single lean year. Winters were mild and snow fell deep, and every harvest seemed richer than the one before. Trade was brisk, the best craftsmen flocked to their markets, and soon Petr didn't know what to do with the money. He built new roads and bridges, churches and convents, gave out dowries and threw public feasts, just because he could, because he felt drunk on power, because there wasn't much else for him to do. There were no challenges at all, no hardships to overcome, no chance to make his name remembered through history.

As a boy he'd always thought he'd lead a conquest after he took the crown, maybe even unite all the Rus under Murom. Now, after years of prosperity, they could muster a force that would be unstoppable. But he'd lost all taste for blood.

His idle army patrolled trade routes, guarded remote villages from the raiders. He did his best to keep them busy, and still his generals spent the first decade of his reign clamouring for a war.

"But why?" Fevronia asked when he complained to her. "What's the point of it?"

"Glory, lands, wealth."

"I don't want you to go."

He didn't either. A campaign would mean months away from home, and he needed to be by her side. Every day there was something important to tell her, something precious to learn about her, and every night with her seemed to bring him closer to something bright and divine.

"Do you want more land?" She reached for the map, and he could almost see trails of fire and destruction spreading where she traced her finger, countless corpses paving way for his triumph.

"No, stop," he pleaded and snatched the map

from her, and she understood, and they never spoke of that again.

He'd thought Fevronia's glow would dull once they returned to the palace, but she seemed as content as she'd been on the day they left Murom together. She'd changed: there was a new mystery and power about her, a soul-deep, sure happiness. It was as if she'd learnt a great secret that day and now felt compassion and pity for all who still stumbled through their lives in the dark.

She wove her craft again: cured the sick, healed the barren, saw women through hard childbirths. When Petr found out he was horrified at first.

"What price did you take from them?" he demanded.

"Nothing. What can they give me? I already have what I want."

Her skill was known far beyond Murom. Pilgrims lined up in rows before their churches, hoping for one touch of her hand as she and Petr walked to prayer. And they didn't come just for her. Murom's churches were favoured by the Blessed: madmen who went into holy frenzies that made all the onlookers see divine light and hear songs of the angels. Whenever Petr and Fevronia walked by all the Blessed had a fit as one.

"Glory, glory!" they yelled in unison, convulsing on the wooden paving before the church. "The exalted one cometh, touched by the light!"

"Friends of yours?" Petr asked Fevronia. "Fellow witches?"

"Shamans. I told them here's a good place for their craft."

Boyars and their wives, townsfolk and the priests all held Fevronia in the highest regard, and nobody questioned the source of her power. Either they couldn't tell what she was, or knew better than to speak out.

"How can they not see?" Petr asked her once. "We've been married for many years, and you've not aged a day. Don't they think it strange?"

She gave him an odd look and turned him toward a mirror.

He saw himself: back bent with age, his hair a colourless grey. By his side was an old woman he didn't recognise. He blinked, surprised, and the glamour faded, and he saw her for what she was: Fevronia, just the same as when he'd first met her.

"Have you enchanted everyone to see you as a crone?"

She laughed and laughed and looked so pleased with herself, so happy.

He was very old. Decades flew by without him noticing. Marfa had remarried once the grieving was done and bore three boys in three years. They were men now, fathers themselves. When he felt it was time he named her eldest, Yuri, his heir.

"You are the greatest knjaz Murom ever had," the new bishop quietly told him at a feast in Yuri's honour. Petr stared at him, startled.

"The land has prospered under you, risen to the glory we'd never known. The years of peace and plenty we've had, the miracles we've seen - your reign was blessed by the Lord. You'll be remembered for centuries."

Fevronia quietly picked at her food, and Petr couldn't look away from her. He knew very well who had blessed his reign. Like a peasant woman would keep her home in order, Fevronia had kept their kingdom safe and thriving for sixty years: for him, out of love, and for herself because the work pleased her.

"Of course we have your wife to thank," said the bishop, and Petr had to put his spoon down to hide the tremble in his hand. "A man is only half a man without a woman. I tell this to every couple I marry: be as Petr and Fevronia, one in body and soul, serve our Lord daily with your love, and you'll be blessed as they are. You've been an example to all the faithful. You two should be the patron saints of Murom."

Later Petr woke in middle of the night, shaken by the hammering of his own heart.

"I'm going to hell," he said.

Fevronia's eyes glowed bright green in the dark. He should have been used to that by now.

"You go where I go," she said.

He'd barely thought of his own soul since they married, and he'd never thought of hers. She seemed unbound by mortal fate, something other than human. But everyone walked under God and she was a woman, a witch, and her soul belonged to the fire.

"I want my soul to be saved," he said. "I want you to be saved, too. But I can't force you."

She shook her head, turned over and fell asleep again, and he stroked her hair and prayed, prayed.

In the morning he told her he'd decided to end his life in a monastery.

"I understand," she said sadly. "Some things are easier in private."

"That's not the reason. I need to give my soul to God. It's not too late, I can still change my fate."

"Petr, you've nothing to fear. I promise you that."

He wasn't afraid any more; he'd had an epiphany sometime in the night, and now he had hope. Fevronia didn't want to surrender herself to faith, or perhaps even couldn't. He still didn't understand the way of her craft and the price she paid for it. But she was his wife, they were one body and soul. He would pray and repent for both of them, atone for all their shared sins, and he might lead both of them to salvation.

"I want this," he said. "Fevronia, please. I know, I promised myself to you, but I need you to let me do this."

"We were children when we struck that bargain," she said and drew him into her arms. "I didn't realise what it'd mean - I only knew I wanted you. I didn't know what I'd get. And now I can't ask for more. Go if you want, but remember, you're still mine. You're still all I want. Don't die without sending a message to me. Wait for my answer, promise me you won't die until you hear from me."

The quiet, slow life of the monastery was just what his aching body and mind needed. He joined the prayers and ate with the rest of the monks, tried to learn their names, talk to them, do what little chores he was given. But he kept falling asleep - even in the temple, even outside, on the garden rows he meant to be weeding. He felt wrapped in a warm pleasant fog, cut off from everyone else, softly, peacefully fading into nothing. His death felt inevitable and right like the death of grass in the autumn, something that had to happen, not a calamity at all.

He couldn't pray as well as he wanted. His greatest sin was having spent his life married to a witch, and he couldn't repent for that - he couldn't even regret it. But prayers brought him calm and clarity, and he knew he was on the right path.

"Have mercy on her, have mercy on us," he muttered, bowing to the floor. His old knees creaked, but he felt no pain.

One morning he woke up knowing he wouldn't get up from his bed. His body was spent, dry and empty, and his spirit was light as goose down, a mist on his lips about to float away.

"Tell Fevronia," he said when the monks found him, and could barely speak after that. He kissed the cross and followed the prayers with slow, bloodless lips, and waited.

There was no word from her. He wanted to let go, rest, face whatever waited for him beyond death. But he'd made her a promise, and he struggled to hold on. Blissful numbness had faded and fiery pain raked now through his body, and his soul was heavy, restless.

He was too weak for this last trial. He'd promised her more than he could give, just like the first time, and now he'd betray her again.

"Have mercy, forgive me," he repeated after the priest. The room grew dark; he couldn't see the cross held right before his face. Fevronia's hare fidgeted in the doorway, nervously drummed on the posts as if rousing itself for a fight.

"Where is she?" Petr asked, and then knew she was here. The darkness around him was laced with green, moving. Thick oak branches grew through the wooden ceiling, stretched toward him; young leaves unfolded before his eyes, a whole week of spring in one breath. The monks weren't alarmed - they didn't see. This was just for him, a message, a promise.

A young monk pushed toward his bed, breathless from a run.

"Fevronia says she's ready," the boy said, and Petr closed his eyes, grateful and calm, and was gone in a single exhale.

He fell into the cool bed of oak leaves and melted into the branches, and Fevronia's arms closed around him.

They drifted together, higher and higher, and the safe shade of green was left behind. There was harsh silver light all around them, bright and beautiful and cruel like fire. It hurt, it meant to burn all of him that had been Petr and leave him clean like an old bone. But Fevronia still held him, and he still existed.

"Glory, glory," the light sang against them. Something kept moving in the blaze, beating around them like enormous wings, thunderous, terrifying. They were in the very heart of light, blind from it. Everything went still, and there was a voice.

Every sound of it shook the world around them, tore Petr's soul open, brought pain and joy beyond endurance. The voice spoke of love, Petr knew that, but could only grasp the last few words.

"What do you want?" the voice asked.

And Fevronia answered, and they went on.

The Gift
by Susi Liarte

Tamsin was lost. The map she held was hand-drawn, because all the others she'd seen only showed the woodland as a plain green block.

"They'll be no use to you," her friend Amy had said. "Even if I tried to write on them, you're better off with landmarks."

So Tamsin stood, staring at a thatch-crossed path instead of the large oak with the three bird boxes she was looking for. It was still mid-morning, so there was no danger of her having to give up and turn back. Clouds sailed slowly overhead, and the high breeze caressed the top of the canopy. The ascending sun glimmered through the leaves of early summer.

All that would change by next year. The land was to be sold and potential developers were already gathering funding and putting together business papers to plan their projects. Even after consultations and protests, none of the options being considered involved keeping the forest as it was. Tamsin had heard of the 'wanderer's shrine' a few times, and she was determined to see it for herself before it disappeared. Amy, of all people, had been there before - she'd joined an end of year ramble where they sat under the trees drinking and had to find their way back at dawn. Even though there was nothing much to see there, Amy admitted that the atmosphere had been pretty special.

Tamsin went right; even without the oak as a landmark, she knew she was heading vaguely northward. Idle thoughts drifted through her mind: maybe she should join a walking group and find other places like this. At some point she'd have to dig into the lunch she'd packed. Wasn't such a forest best left as it was? There wasn't much someone like her could do.

A bird flitted across her path and made her jump. The forest was quiet except for distant sounds and she became aware of her breathing. The further she went into the natural space the more she'd have to be careful not to disturb the wildlife. It seemed fairly obvious where people had walked and where they hadn't, but that didn't mean it was hers to inhabit. She felt a pang of protectiveness for the woods - her footsteps were trivial compared to the machines that would arrive to cut the whole place down. Although it hadn't happened yet. Perhaps some wildlife agency would find some funding and put in a massive bid. It didn't seem like it would work like that, but she wanted to think that the protests had touched someone's heart.

"Oh! *There* you are," Tamsin said to the grand oak as it came into view. She gazed at it for a moment before getting her phone out to take a picture. In the end, she took three. She checked the time and then slipped the phone back in her pocket.

Tamsin wanted to sit with it for a while. She was making good time, and there was no reason to rush in a place like this. She sat beneath it, making a seat of its big, solid roots, and leaned against the trunk. *Hello and goodbye*, Tamsin thought. It was like meeting a stranger and sharing a smile, knowing you'll never see them again. For that brief moment, it would be her shrine to the world, a place where she could rest at one with it, and feel like she belonged. She uncapped her water bottle and took a sip, looking around. A blackbird hopped nearby, keeping a wary distance. Tamsin was hoping for a squirrel or even a stray cat that had made its home here. Once again, her heart filled with worry about what would happen to all this.

Well, moping wouldn't help. She got up and dusted her jeans off, and soon continued on her way. The oak was the final landmark before the shrine, so she looked all around her as she walked. The only description Amy could give was 'stones' with a vague hand gesture towards the ground.

The path was more defined now, or it seemed that way from the flowers growing either side. They led Tamsin through a different kind of beauty than had surrounded the oak; this one more vibrant, more riotous, as if summer was emanating from a concentrated source. Tamsin stopped. She could feel the atmosphere Amy had mentioned. A good feeling.

Tamsin heard a soft whisper. It wasn't sharp like the rustling of leaves above, but there was still a little room for doubt.

"Hello?" Tamsin cleared her throat.

"Will you help?" The words overlapped each other like a single breath.

Tamsin shivered. She was sure enough of her own senses to know there was no person or loudspeaker behind a tree. Voices in the forest were not something she felt prepared to comprehend at that moment.

"You are kind." The female voice was warm, a vibration between the earth and sunbeams. Intangible as the air where the dust motes danced.

"What is this?" Tamsin was rooted to the ground, her own voice hushed in awe.

"My sisters and I have looked after this forest for a long time." The voice still seemed to echo, but the words were more distinct. "I have come to understand. Soon there will be nothing to protect."

"You want me... to save you?"

"We will endure. We can make things grow, but

not fast enough to counteract this. Like the birds that fly south, I will have nowhere to return to."

Tamsin shook her head and took a deep breath. She took her water bottle out for a swig. "Look... even if you are real, I can't do anything about it."

"I understand."

Was that the end of it? Tamsin stood still, breathing, waiting. She sighed. "Where is the shrine?"

The sunlight pulsed with the response. "You wish to make an offering?"

"I think-"

"To those who would spoil this place?"

Tamsin blinked. She hadn't really thought of leaving anything valuable, but others probably had. If the shrine was dug up, it wouldn't exactly be done by the intended recipient. "Who are you?"

"You may call me Aestas."

"Do you have a body?"

"Not like yours."

Silly question to ask an ethereal being. "Right."

"I will show you the place you seek."

Tamsin took a moment to check she was still in the land of the living; she squeezed her little finger with her other hand and then got out her phone. Not much time had passed. She could turn back, but she wasn't afraid. Sceptical, a little. If the voice started to try to make a deal she would be out of there. She moved forward slowly, and just off the path was a little clearing. She could see the stones, some large, others small and knocked to the ground. She had a sofa chair bigger than this. Around it, the scattering of dried flowers but also discarded bottles.

She felt sorry for the spirit. "They're not exactly offerings, you know."

"It is a memory of their revelry. There was an old man who tended this shrine, but he has passed on, as the seasons do."

Tamsin knelt down and righted a few stones, along with a wooden bowl she found face down in the soil. A few insects skittered from under it. "I have a bag. I can pick them up."

"Take it all."

"I'll clean the litter. But even if this place does go... I can't bring myself to desecrate a shrine."

"It will be rubble."

"We don't know that! They might see it, and..." Tamsin looked down. It still didn't look like much. "...keep it." She sighed, unconvinced. Tamsin shifted so she was cross-legged, and contemplated. After a few minutes she dug her lunch out of her bag, and ate. A large crow flew down and perched atop the tallest stone. It cocked its head at her. "M'not givin' you any food," she said through a mouthful. When she didn't move, it flapped down to the ground and started poking its beak behind the shrine. Tamsin watched it. It was still digging and tugging at something by the time she finished her sandwich and she peered at it, wanting to help but unwilling to startle it. Eventually, there was the soft crumpling of paper and the crow hopped backwards with its prize. It gave Tamsin another round of scrutiny and then flapped forward to leave it beside her before flying up and away to the safety of the branches. "Thank you!" Tamsin called.

It was an old, soil-covered envelope, scrunched up around the shape of an object inside.

Tamsin turned it over. She could barely make out the name on the front: 'Beatrice'.

"What, am I supposed to open it now?"

No one answered.

Despite her curiosity, Tamsin stood. She wasn't in the mood for any more surprises. "I'm going."

The crow's caw was her only response. She stowed the letter in her coat pocket and looked around to make sure she hadn't missed any litter. She felt a little bereft, but also relieved that she no longer had to decide what to believe. The voice might have been a dream, but the object was real, and the bird and the stones and the sunlight. She walked back down the path, the flowers not seeming as vibrant as before. When she reached the oak tree, she walked around it, searching for any sign that would help her make sense of it all. It stood with the same serene dignity as before, and Tamsin found comfort in that.

"Goodbye."

The coffee shop was Tamsin's go-to happy place. The chatter of customers and the hiss of the coffee machine anchored her back to normality.

Hey Amy, she texted, *did you ever find anything weird in that forest?* She unfolded a paper napkin and placed the envelope on top.

Her phone pinged. *No, why? What did you find?*

Just a letter. At least that's what she assumed it was. Only one way to find out.

Then post it.

There was hand sanitiser nearby; Tamsin was sure she'd need to use it. She slipped her thumb under the edge of the envelope but it opened easily. Inside was a small cloth bundle the size of her palm, and a folded piece of paper. It felt brittle, and Tamsin could only imagine it had been there for some time. The handwriting was faint, as if the tree it was under had sucked it of its ink. She could just make out the date. *1921.* Tamsin inhaled sharply.

Dearest Betsy,
I must first apologise for the disappointment you must feel in finding a letter after I promised to meet you. I dare not write to your house and risk exposing you to your family's remarks. I hope you will think to look in our usual

place for news. It is with the heaviest heart that I must tell you I depart to-morrow. There is nothing I want less than to be parted from you. One promise, however, I will not break. I intended to give you the enclosed gift in person, but now that cannot be so, know that it was my mother's. I hope you will wear it and think of me until I can return. I will think of you, and pray that you will find a way to follow your heart.
 Yours always,
 Aurélie

Tamsin stared at the neat writing, and found herself starting to read the letter again from the top. Whatever had happened to either of them must have been a tragedy, if their forbidden love wasn't tragic enough. The letter was never found, and yet, why was Tamsin the one who held it? She put the letter back in the envelope and picked up the gift. If she could find out who these people were, maybe she could return it. She unwrapped the square of fabric and noticed it was a handkerchief, embroidered with the initials *A.B.* Not a surname, but more than she had a moment ago. The tissue paper crumbled in her hands and she parted it to reveal an ornate silver brooch, with pearls and blue stones dotted like flowers. Aestas might have given her this, but Tamsin knew it was never meant for her. Her heart was pounding a bit, but she knew she had to at least try.

The library wasn't far, and there she could search the local census database. There was one very obvious entry, Aurélie Bellemont, that seemed to match what she was looking for. Once she had the name, she found out there was still family in the area, and got hold of the address.

It was late afternoon. Tamsin stood outside the townhouse and double checked she was in the right place. If she handed the letter in and walked away, would she be satisfied?

She rang the doorbell.

A man who looked to be in his thirties opened the door. "Yes?"

"Hi, are you... George Richardson?"

"I am."

"I have something that belongs to your family. I think. A letter written by your great aunt, Aurélie."

He blinked at her. "Really? All right." He held his hand out, his movement uncertain.

It seemed impertinent to ask what had happened to Aurélie all those years ago, so she gave him the napkin-wrapped envelope and smiled.

He paused with his hand on the door and deliberated for a moment. "Would you like to come in? You can tell me how you have this."

"Right." Tamsin would have to omit the part about the voice in the woods, but the rest she could tell. "I found it in the forest. It was wedged between the roots of a tree."

George offered her some tea, but she declined. He sat opposite her and opened the bundle curiously. Tamsin had probably worn the exact same expression - searching, disbelieving - when she had unwrapped it herself. The clock ticked loudly as he read. "Wow. How did you even-" He shook his head. "Thank you for bringing this to me."

"Well, it's been an unusual day. I knew it wasn't an ordinary find."

"I have to give you something for it." He got up and went to the large mahogany desk in the corner, and pulled out a chequebook.

"No, I don't need money!" Tamsin said, standing up.

George shook his head. "Look- What's your name?"

She felt a flush rise to her face. "Tamsin."

"Tamsin, do you know how much sapphires are worth? You could have sold it, but you didn't. It's the least I can do. What's your surname?"

"Rowland."

He wrote out the cheque and then tore it out for her. "Here."

She hesitated, but took it from him. "Three thousand pounds!?"

George shrugged. "It's an unusual day for me too, you know. It seemed a reasonable amount."

"What... Can you just tell me what happened to Aurélie?"

"He was my grandfather's younger sister. On my mother's side. As you can probably tell from the name, that part of the family was French. I know she married someone there."

"Do you know anything about Betsy?"

George shook his head. "No. But I can try to find out. I can get in touch with you if I do, if that helps."

A soft chime marked the hour.

"Thanks. I should probably go." It was five o'clock. Everything would be closing soon. She should go to a bank. "Thanks for... for this." Tamsin still felt she didn't deserve that sum of money, but if he had it spare, she couldn't feel bad forever. He had made a good point regarding the sale value. It was probably worth a lot more.

"Not at all. Thank *you*. I'll see you out."

It was a short walk into town. That morning, she'd been thinking about what would be lost, and now she had gained so much. She stopped in the middle of the pavement, remembering Aesta's voice. The council offices were just across the road, and Tamsin's thoughts all lined up. If she ran, she could make it in time before they closed.

"Hello," she said breathlessly at the counter.

"How may I help you?"

"Do you know how much woodland I can buy with three thousand pounds?"

The staff member looked surprised. "Let me just check that for you." She typed on her keyboard for a few moments. "You'd have to make an appointment with that department, but I believe that would be about half an acre."

That was plenty. "Can you book me in, please? Tamsin Rowland. I'd like to put in an application."

For the Trees
by Cathryn Burge

Seed

The Jobcentre had been a disaster. Louis slapped the information pack they'd forced on him onto the table with, he felt, enough drama to convey his exasperation without overdoing it, thereby ruining his chances of getting sympathy for his awful fate.

"I ask you – *me*?" he sighed. "A forestry apprentice? What do *I* know about forestry?"

Em was in the comfy chair by the fire, absorbed a crossword. She looked up, distracted.

"Hmmm? What's up, babe?"

"Everything!" Now he had her full attention, Louis flung himself onto the sofa and threw an arm across his forehead. "I mean, I may own a checked shirt and a pair of Timberlands, but that does *not* make me a lumberjack, does it? I mean - *does it*?"

Em gaped. As well she might. "They found you a job?"

"Yes." Louis' jaw clenched in horror. "They found me a job. In forestry." It was awful. Terrible. He'd never wielded an axe in his life, nor shouted 'timber!' or done any of the other macho things loggers did. He fluttered his eyelashes at Em imploringly. He deserved some recompense for his upcoming ordeal, surely? "I'm in shock, Em. I need tea."

"Me, too," she said. "Thanks."

That was *not* what he'd meant and she knew it. She was supposed to have fussed over him and agreed that the Jobcentre woman was beyond evil for even *mentioning* forestry, let alone arranging an interview. Instead, she was behaving as if it were no big deal. Louis narrowed his eyes at her. It was all right for Ms Smarty Pants with her Double First in looking cute (and, okay, her *actual* Double First): she was always walking into cushy jobs. Working in the woods would be dangerous. There'd be chainsaws, and ropes, and massive tree trunks to haul about - all in the company of men with enormous arms and an ungodly number of tattoos. It was suddenly clear to Louis that he should have worked harder at uni. Harder at secondary school. Dear God, he should probably have passed up on the sandpit at primary school and got down to some serious early years study.

"There might be wolves," he grumbled – mostly to himself, since Em was so heartless. "Or bears."

"You *like* bears," she said.

Louis glared. How dare she bring up Tom at at time like this? And that hadn't exactly gone well, had it? Tom had broken Louis' heart and Louis had sworn off blokes like him ever since.

He heaved himself up from the sofa and stomped off to the kitchen, determined to put sugar in her tea instead of sweeteners. She'd have trouble waltzing into PR jobs if she was three hundred pounds. He turned the tap on full and watched water gush into the sink, splashing the walls and worktop; then he filled the kettle and slammed it down onto its stand. God damn it, he was going to feed her biscuits, too.

He was just reaching into her Hormonal Emergencies stash (Chocolate Hobnobs, Jaffa Cakes) when she appeared in the kitchen doorway, his information pack in hand.

"It's not going to be like *Axe Men*, you know," she

said. "From what it says here -" She tapped the top page. "- it's more about woodland management. Environmental monitoring. Science-y stuff."

"And just what do I know about science?" Louis snapped. Behind him, the kettle came to a rattling boil, sounding as angry as he felt. "I have a degree in Fine Arts."

"You have a *third* in Art History," Em countered, never shy of pointing out the disparity between their academic achievements in order to win an argument. "It was hardly your vocation."

"Cow," Louis hissed.

"Drama queen."

In Louis' book, the only reasonable response to that was to scowl, huff and toss his head.

Em ignored him and finished making the tea. When she was done she came over and hugged him.

"Chill," she said, and kissed his cheek. "You've got to get through the interview first - and, even if they take you on, they're not going to want to keep you, are they?"

Selection

Amazingly, the interview location was not half-way up a mountain, miles from civilisation. It was in the centre of town, just a street away from Lush and Diesel. Louis hesitated outside the office block with its tinted windows and stainless steel nameplates, trying to crush the kernel of hope that was threatening to take root somewhere between his stomach and his throat: even if the job didn't turn out to be utterly shit, he wasn't qualified for it. He'd never so much as mown a lawn, for God's sake.

He went in.

And quickly realized the building was only an employment agency. The girl on reception was better groomed than he was – and he'd made a serious effort to create the right impression: his one and only good suit (Armani and a graduation/get-a-job gift from Granny in charcoal wool), pale blue shirt (Tommy Hilfilger, a Christmas present from Tom before he sodded off with that muscled moron from his kickboxing class) and ginger suede loafers (Magnanni, and major contributors to the massive student debt he'd be paying off until the end of time). Obviously, the impression he was aiming for was that of a determined city-dweller with an allergy to getting his hands dirty. To press the point home, he'd given himself a thorough manicure as well.

The receptionist checked his name against a list on her computer.

"Louis Allsopp for Bob Dukes from Silvis PLC - room twenty-four, second floor. The lift is over there," she said, pointing.

She had the most magnificent nails.

Bob Dukes: the name said it all and, as the lift purred upwards, Louis pictured someone stocky and balding, wearing horrible clothes. Dukes would probably have a Northern accent as well, and be the sort who prided himself on calling a spade a spade.

He wasn't. He was gorgeous; everything about him exquisite. He was tall, lean and fit with fine facial features, framed by loose dark curls. As for his eyes, they were so blue under those long sooty lashes, they ought to have come with a Risk of Drowning warning. Definitely *not* a bear. Just in time, Louis remembered it was unattractive to drool.

"Mr Allsopp," Bob said, and his handshake was perfect, too. Just the right amount of pressure, warm and dry. "I'm Bob Dukes. Thank you for coming."

Louis opened his mouth but nothing came out. He tried again. "Call me Louis," he said and deployed his most appealing smile. Suddenly he wanted this job. Wanted it badly.

Cruelly, Bob released his hand to indicate a chair. "Please, sit down ... Louis."

Louis sank onto the black leather cushions, knees mostly useless thanks to the way Bob had said his name. If nothing else came of this interview, at least he'd have some new fantasy material to work with.

"It says here you went to Falchester," Bob said, referring to Louis' details on his computer screen. "Day boy or boarder?"

"Boarder," Louis groaned. "I hated it."

Bob leaned forward. "Awful, wasn't it? Was the rugby team still a bunch of Neanderthals in your day?"

" 'My day' can't have been more than five years after yours," Louis said. "Neanderthal evolution takes longer than that."

A sense of camaraderie born of shared horror bloomed warm between them and they both relaxed. Bob asked a few desultory questions about Louis' background and work experience, as well as his understanding of what forestry work entailed, and Louis tried to give sensible answers, even though half the time he was just watching Bob's lips move.

"Well," Bob said at last, "I don't suppose many people would see you and forestry as an obvious fit, but I like you. You're smart and you seem like a fast learner. However, business is business and I'm afraid I can't give you the job just like that."

Thoughts of offering special favours flashed, not unpleasantly, through Louis' mind, but Bob was still speaking.

"I'll give you a two-week trial," he said, "to convince me I want you."

Germination

The following Monday, at stupid o'clock, Louis found himself scowling at a pallet of saplings. He'd envisaged himself in a more desk-type role, like Bob - maybe advising on office *décor* and colour schemes - not digging holes on a wind-swept, rain-lashed hillside. In his work-issue waterproofs, he was simultaneously too hot and too cold, body sweating whilst his face and hands froze. *And* he'd torn a nail.

Worse still, Bob was nowhere to be seen. Instead, Louis had been given over to the not-so-tender mercies of foreman Darren Statham. They hadn't exactly hit it off. Louis should never have trusted the warmth of Darren's welcome-to-the-team smile or the twinkle in his eyes: the man had absolutely no sense of humour. Everyone else laughed when Louis grimaced at the well worn spade Darren had given him, saying, "I'm not sure I fancy working with another man's tool", but Darren's face took on a look like thunder.

Darren was the polar opposite of Louis: a gruff, outdoorsy type whom personal grooming had pretty much passed by. His auburn hair was a nice enough colour but completely lacked shape or style, and his eyebrows were in urgent need of tweezing. As for his other facial hair, well, there was stubble and *stubble*, as even the more cursory of glances at *GQ* would have told him if he'd bothered to look. Then again, Darren didn't strike Louis as much of a reader: his conversation was mostly low grunts, narrowed eyes and one-word orders.

And whenever Louis looked round, he seemed to be watching him. Probably planning his murder.

Louis pushed the hair out of his eyes and scanned the hill: he'd need help if Darren really did try to kill him. Adam and Elliot were busy unloading more pallets from the truck, and Scott was digging planting holes like a fiend. He'd managed twenty in the time it had taken Louis to dig two. Determined not to be put to shame, Louis backfilled his second hole as per Darren's demonstration and firmed the soil down about the sapling with the toe of his boot. He knew he'd have to work faster if he wanted to keep this job, but he wasn't sure he did. Without Bob around for motivation, it was hard to see the point.

For the time being, however, he was stuck. They'd left civilization behind at the motorway junction and the only transport out was Darren's minibus, with its Man Smell and rock-hard seats. There would be no getting off site until the end of the day. Louis might as well get on with it and hope that Bob came out.

Bob didn't. At the end of the day, it was Darren who came strolling up the hill like a forty-five degree incline was nothing to see how Louis had done. His conclusion: not very well, but not badly enough to warrant getting the sack. Louis didn't know whether to feel triumphant or wretched as he climbed up into the minibus; he was mostly too tired to care.

He must have fallen asleep en route home because, suddenly, the bus had come to a halt and it was just him and Darren left inside.

"Pick you up tomorrow at six-thirty," Darren said as Louis stumbled out onto the pavement.

"I'll be dead before then."

One corner of Darren's mouth twitched. "You'll live," he said. "The job's never killed anyone before."

Louis took a step in the direction of his house, wincing at the effort. "Yeah, well I may be the exception that proves the rule."

"Six-thirty," Darren said. "Don't be late."

The hundred yards from where Darren dropped him off to home felt worse than cross-country at school. Louis lumbered up the front path and let himself in.

The house was like another world: warm, and soft, and smelling of bath bombs. Louis prised off his boots, let his jacket lie where it fell and staggered into the living room.

Em was at the crossword puzzles again, this time cosy in her dressing gown and slippers.

"Well, look at you," she said, bright eyes darting over Louis, taking everything in. "The working man, home from the hills."

"The *ravenous* working man," Louis said and claimed the sofa, sprawling out so that he was almost fully prone, head propped up on Em's *Iron Man* cushion. "There was no canteen and I'd eaten all my sandwiches by ten. What's for dinner?"

Em gave him A Look.

"One: this is not the nineteen-fifties. Two: I am not your wife. And three: technically, it's your turn to cook."

"Technically? Do I smell a loop-hole?"

"You smell, full stop." Em wrinkled her nose. "God, they really made you work, didn't they?"

"In *overalls*. It was ghastly."

Em set her crossword and pen down on the coffee table, and stood up. "Poor baby. Tell you what, just this once, I'll order a takeaway."

Growth

An almighty thump, followed by a blood-curling scream, wrenched Louis from sleep. It sounded like Em was being murdered. The battering continued as he tried to make sense of it but Em had gone eerily silent. Louis leapt out of bed. She might be past hope but he was still alive, with every intention of staying that way. He needed to run - and fast.

He could scarcely move. Everything ached. Every muscle was tight, the fibres grating over one another as he tried to flee. He hobbled across the bedroom floor, threw open the door and lurched onto the landing.

And crashed straight into Em.

"You bastard!" she screeched, raining down slaps on him. "I don't need to be up 'til eight!"

Louis grabbed her wrists in self-defence. "Wha-?"

His almost-question was answered by yet more banging. Downstairs. At the front door.

He swallowed, his brain finally catching up. "Oh."

" 'Oh' indeed," Em spat and shook herself free of his grip. "Are you going to get that? Before he breaks the door down?"

Louis wanted nothing more than to crawl back into bed, but the idea of risking Em's wrath was worse than facing Darren's so he dragged himself stairs-ward, as Em huffed loudly behind him and flounced back into her room.

Opening the front door let in a cold blast of November air. It hit Louis' bed-warm skin so hard it took his breath away. Goosepimples sprouted on his arms and chest, his nipples pulled tight and - *shit* - Darren was getting an eyeful.

He didn't appear to be enjoying it.

"Get dressed," he said, looking quickly away. "You've got quarter of an hour while I pick up the others."

It was on the tip of Louis' tongue to ask what they had that he didn't, but Darren's tight jaw forestalled him. He went to get dressed.

Half-way through the morning, Louis was starving. After getting up so early, he'd had no appetite for breakfast, and Darren's fifteen minute reprieve was hardly enough to get showered and dressed, let alone make sandwiches. Plus he'd forgotten he needed them. He'd never needed to plan before, never been so far from a Starbucks.

God, he hated forestry.

Returning to the pallet for his next sapling, he noticed Adam and Elliot had downed tools. A delicious aroma of coffee wafted up on the breeze and Louis thought he'd sell his soul for even half a cupful.

It took him a while to realize that Elliot was holding up his thermos flask and waving. He seemed to want Louis to join him. Hoping against hope, Louis left his saplings to fend for themselves and, ignoring Darren's ever watchful scrutiny, stumbled down the hillside. Adam and Elliot had barely spoken two words to him yesterday and they hadn't seemed too impressed with his time-keeping this morning, either. He couldn't quite believe they were willing to share.

But Elliot pressed the thermos into his unbelieving hands, saying, "Hang on - I've got a spare cup somewhere in my bag."

Louis felt like sinking to his knees in gratitude. Though obviously not in *that* way. Although ... he watched Elliot bend over his rucksack to rummage around inside and decided the man had quite a nice arse. And thighs. Maybe Louis had been too hasty in dismissing him, and since Bob wasn't around-

"Here."

If Louis hadn't been still racked with pain from the previous day's labours on top of today's, he might have jumped at the voice behind him. As it was, he turned stiffly to see Adam holding out a caramel Rocky.

Louis fell on it. The chocolate was bliss and his

whole world shrank down to the velvet texture of it melting in his mouth. Plus caramel and biscuit! Louis decided he might well be in love.

Adam chuckled, and Louis realized he must have involuntarily closed his eyes. He snapped them open, feeling ridiculous and vulnerable, certain Adam and Elliot were going to take the piss out of him mercilessly.

"Forgot to bring anything on my second day, too," Adam said. "Too bloody knackered to think about anything but bed when I got home. How're you finding it?"

"Hideous."

Adam laughed.

"Yeah," Elliot said. "It can be. On jobs like this. They really threw you in at the deep-end, didn't they?"

The coffee must have been doing its good work, because Louis found his brain was suddenly back online.

"Jobs like this? There are others?"

"Oh, yeah. There's plenty of variety. Planting's the worst."

"Second worst," Adam corrected.

"What's the worst?"

"Felling. But they mostly get contractors in for that."

Maybe it was the coffee, or the biscuit, or even the social interaction but Louis felt a flicker of optimism trying to catch alight inside him. This wasn't the whole of the job. There might be bits of it he liked. Bits that might even mean involve seeing Bob.

Stem

Mid-afternoon, a red dot in the distance caught Louis' attention. A couple of minutes later, he identified it as a sports car, snaking its way along the valley. As it got closer, he could tell it was a Jaguar, and a brand-new one at that.

The car turned off the main road and down the fork to where Darren had parked the minibus. Louis watched it pull up and a tall, dark-haired bloke got out. At first, he was just a vaguely interesting stranger. Then Louis' heart-rate picked up. It was Bob, only not wearing his sharp office suit but jeans and an oatmeal jumper. He looked *amazing*.

Sadly, instead of coming straight up to Louis, Bob made a bee-line for Darren and they were soon locked in intense conversation. Darren got out his tablet and showed it to Bob; Bob studied whatever was on it for a while, then clapped Darren warmly on the shoulder, letting his hand rest there for longer than Louis felt strictly necessary. Envy lanced through him. He would have given anything to be in Darren's place – but did Darren appreciate it? No, he did not. His whole body stiffened and he took a step back. Then he was talking again, stabbing at his tablet with a forefinger. He'd raised his voice, too, though not enough for Louis to catch what he was saying. Suddenly, both Bob and Darren turned and looked up the hill. Louis was sure they were talking about him – and then that they weren't. Why would they be? He was just the useless trainee forced on them by the Jobcentre. Except–

Bob had left Darren behind and was striding up the hill. Louis tried telling himself he must want to speak to Adam, or Scott, but no: he walked right past them with no more than a wave. Louis tightened his grip on his spade. Whatever Darren had been saying, it hadn't looked good. A return to unemployment was surely looming.

Windswept, Bob looked younger, his eyes even brighter. There was a slight pinkness to his cheeks from the cold and the effort of climbing the hill, but it was a good look on him, emphasizing the colour of his lips and, as he came right up close, Louis found himself licking his own.

"Hello, Louis," Bob said. "How are you're getting on?"

Louis swallowed. Why didn't he have one of his trademark sassy answers on the tip of his tongue, instead of a lame, "Maybe you should tell me."

Bob cast a glance down at Darren. "I'd say you're doing ... okay."

"I am?"

"Planting's back-breaking work. It takes a while to get into your stride. You'll get there."

Louis could scarcely believe his ears. "Is that what Darren said?"

Bob snorted. "Not exactly."

Louis shuffled his feet. "I'm trying, Bob. Really, I am."

Bob sighed. "Listen, I took a chance hiring you. I need you to pick up the pace."

"I will!" Louis' promise came out far too quickly and too loud. He cringed at the desperation in it.

"Okay," Bob said, "so let's make a deal. I keep you on and you work faster. Tell me I can rely on you -" Bob paused, looked down, then up again. "- to keep your end up."

Louis' heart thudded at Bob's phrasing, at the hint of a promise behind it, but he reined himself in. No cheeky riposte this time, just eager sincerity. He placed his hand over his heart in an echo of the gesture that accompanied the Falchester pledge.

"I will, Bob," he said. "Absolutely, I will."

Snag

The next morning, Louis was still on a high from his chat with Bob and he positively sashayed down the front path, belly fluttering, heart hopeful. Bob was going to make a move soon, he was sure, and he flashed Darren a dazzling smile as he approached the minibus.

Darren didn't smile back. He barely even grunted hello when Louis opened the door and climbed in.

"Six twenty-six," Louis said, tapping his watch. He wanted his effort to be on time acknowledged. It was cold and dark, and he was facing another freezing day on the hill; he wasn't used to this life but he was trying.

"Six twenty-nine," Darren said, without looking at him and shoved the bus into gear.

A second minibus was on the parking site when Darren pulled up, its occupants, clad in Silvis overalls, already spilling out into the frosty dawn. Four more blokes, all of them fit and built; one impressively tall. Had Louis realized forestry would offer such a boxful of eye candy, he might have tried it sooner.

With his usual charm, Darren set about making the introductions. Louis vaguely registered the names (Daniel, Matt, Ryan) but his attention was on the tall one – Josh - who was disturbingly square-jawed and handsome. Inevitably, Louis felt a tickle of attraction but he was also slightly put out. Until now, he'd been the best-looking in this group; he didn't appreciate being faced with competition. But it was clear from Josh's manner that he didn't even think there was any. He gave Louis' hand a polite but bored shake and headed off to the tool stack.

Meanwhile, Daniel and Matt started loading more pallets onto the four-by-four's trailer whilst Ryan and Josh made their way up to Louis' spot on the hill.

"Hey!" Louis said.

Darren thrust a spade into his hand. "Hey *what*?"

Louis felt stupid. It wasn't his spot. He didn't care about it; he didn't care about the *job*. Why the hell was he feeling so affronted?

"That's where I was working," he said, aiming for tough and manly but sounding pouty and pathetic instead.

"That's what you call it, is it?" Darren gave a short, hard laugh. "Thirty trees planted in two days."

"I'm doing my best!"

Darren face softened. He sighed and scrubbed a hand through his hair. "Yeah," he said. "You probably are."

"So you've replaced me? After two days?" Heat was rising under Louis' skin. He'd never worked so hard in his life.

"You're not replaced," Darren said. "You're just moved. That bit of the slope is too difficult for someone so unfit. I want you over there." He pointed to a far more gentle incline, where the grass was white with frost. "But I want to see your work rate double."

Louis was tempted to give him the spade back and suggest somewhere painful he could stick it, but he settled for some furious glowering.

Which, for some reason, made Darren smile, revealing surprisingly attractive dimples that disappeared down into his stubble and even, white teeth.

"*Double* your work rate," he said.

The new saplings Louis had been tasked with planting were much smaller, and came with protective plastic tubes. They were light and easy to lift, and required far less digging to plant. They also needed more delicate handling to avoid damaging their roots. They were an insult, Louis was sure, and he would have stamped all over them out of spite, but it wasn't the trees' fault Darren hated him.

After a while, he settled into a rhythm, his spade cutting neat squares through the grass, moss and soil. By coffee time, his section was bristling with grey-green tubing. The sight gave him a strange rush of satisfaction. One day, those tiny saplings would be part of a forest, strong trees he had planted rising up to meet the sky. He reached for his thermos: it was a thought that need toasting with something warm and sweet.

As he drank, looking out over the wintry valley, Darren joined him, clutching a coffee of his own. In the distance, Bob's red Jag was approaching. Louis knew he must be grinning like an idiot when he turned to see what Darren wanted but he didn't care.

For a moment, Darren's face was a picture of confusion, then he cleared his throat and diverted his gaze to Louis' scrap of land.

"How many?" he asked. It was obviously A Lot but it would probably have killed him to offer praise.

"Twenty," Louis said, with another little swell of pride.

Darren sipped at his coffee. "Better."

"*And* I've got blisters."

Louis pulled off a glove to show him the full agony of it but Darren was profoundly unimpressed.

"Come with the job," he said. "Better get used to them."

Brilliant. Not only did Louis get to freeze his balls off and break his back on this job, he'd also get to wreck his beautiful, artist's hands as well. Though, wait a moment, 'better get used to them' must mean

...
"Are you saying you've decided to keep me on?" he asked, very nearly in shock.

Bob's car was a lot closer now; turning off the road and into the parking space.

"I'm saying you're doing better than you were and if ..."

But Louis was only half-listening: Bob had climbed out of his car, wearing a parka short enough to reveal the curve of his bum, and Louis was awash with feeling - pride, anticipation and desire. He raised his hand in greeting.

Bob turned away.

Wait! What? Why? Louis was dizzy with incomprehension as Bob walked over to the new guys, then positively queasy when he clasped Josh in a warm embrace. It was a too-long moment of too-wide smiles and it left Louis reeling.

"What the hell?" he muttered, stricken. "Are they ... *friends*?"

"Something like that," Darren said, and drained his coffee.

And that was that: conversation over. Louis probed a bit, as casually as he could, but Darren was infuriatingly unforthcoming. Back at work, Louis seethed with jealousy. He drove his spade into the ground hard, and stomped it in deeper for good measure. Planted tree after tree after tree. Sweat built on his forehead, despite the cold weather, and his body grew hot. Eventually, he ran out of things to plant.

Everyone else was still hard at it – everyone except Bob. He had his laptop balanced on the bonnet of his car and was leaning over it, providing Louis with a mouth-watering view of his thighs and that shapely backside. It was the backside that made up his mind. As a general rule, he expected to be courted, not to make the running himself but, with Josh on the scene, there wasn't a moment to lose. Louis needed to make his interest clear; make Bob an offer he couldn't refuse. The sex gods apparently approved of this plan: they'd thoughtfully arranged for Louis' next pallet of saplings to be situated right next to Bob's car.

At Louis' approach, Bob looked up and blinked, like his mind was elsewhere.

He snapped his laptop shut. "Did you want something?"

"More saplings," Louis said. "Can't ever have enough wood. If you know what I mean."

That had Bob visibly zooming back to the here and now. He straightened up and smiled.

"My thoughts exactly," he said.

It was now or never. Louis took a deep breath.

"Want to look into that with me on Saturday?" he said.

Felling

Finally – finally! - it was Friday. Just one more day on the hill and then the weekend, Saturday night and *Bob*. It wasn't just the mint shower gel that was making Louis' skin tingle. He turned the radio up and sang along.

Em bashed the wall.

"Don't be afraid to catch the feels, ride drop top and chase the thrills," Louis warbled back at her. He was being a dick, he knew, but he was happy and he had to let it bubble out.

"I hope he turns out to be an axe-murderer and chops you into pieces!" Em yelled as Louis made his way back to his room.

Smiling, he blew a kiss at her bedroom door.

Darren was early with the van but Louis was earlier, stamping his feet on the pavement against the cold.

"Good morning, Mr Statham!" he said, jumping up onto the passenger seat. "And may I say how very handsome you're looking today."

"What the hell?" Darren spluttered and coughed, his cheeks turning red with the effort of not choking.

"What? I can't be excited about going to work?"

"You *can* ..." Darren pushed the van into gear. "It's just, usually, you're not."

Louis debated the wisdom of sharing his news for all of two seconds. He was desperate to talk about it, to tell someone other than Em.

"Big weekend coming up," he said. "I've got a date."

Darren floored the accelerator and the van shot off with a squeal of tyres.

"Aren't you going to ask who with?"

"None of my business," Darren said, gaze dead ahead, hands tight on the wheel.

"We're making *conversation*. Where I tell you things and you tell me things." Louis leant in and whispered. "It's with Bob. Your turn."

"You're an even a bigger idiot than you look," Darren said, and rounded the corner towards Elliot's house so hard, the manoeuvre threw Louis away from him and into the door.

Darren was in a filthy mood all morning. He kept coming over to Louis to tell him he was planting his saplings all wrong: too shallow, too deep, not enough water. It was pretty dispiriting but Louis' dwindling cheer was rescued when Bob appeared and gestured Louis over to his car.

"I can't stay long," he said, speaking an undertone even though no-one else was near enough to hear. It felt deliciously naughty. "I just wanted to firm up our plans for tomorrow night."

Louis grinned. "Firming up's definitely in my plan," he said.

"Right -" Bob dropped his voice lower still, which was dead sexy in a cloak-and-dagger kind of way. "- I'll pick you up from your place at seven and take you to mine."

"You can take me anywhere," Louis said.

The final pallet of saplings was empty. Darren called a meeting near the tools container to review the job. According to Elliot, this was a thing he always did, awarding the best performing employee a bottle of Scotch. Annoyingly, the bloke who got to brandish the Glenmorangie was Josh. Darren ran down the rest of the team's results; Louis came last and was surprised to find he cared enough to feel insulted by the look of disappointment on Darren's face.

"I'm new at this," he hissed. "Or maybe it's your crap training."

Darren's nostrils flared. "First and last get to load the empty pallets onto the trailers. Everybody else, clear up any rubbish and put the tools in the vans."

Great. Some one-on-one time with golden boy. Louis couldn't wait. He didn't like Josh; hadn't forgotten that hug Bob had given him.

Predictably, Josh hefted pallets onto his trailer without breaking sweat whilst Louis panted and heaved and thought his back might break.

"Bend at the knees," Josh said, all muscled shoulders and sculpted thighs. "Like this."

He crouched, lifted a pallet and swung it onto the stack on the trailer in one strong, smooth motion.

"Yeah, yeah," Louis said dismissively. "You spend your life in the gym."

He squatted down to seize another pallet and added it to his stack. It didn't land quite square but it was near enough.

Josh lifted another pallet, and positioned that one perfectly, too.

"They need to line up with the sides of the trailer," he said.

"I'm not an idiot. I *know*."

"Just trying to help," Josh said and Louis could hear the shrug in his voice. Good. Perhaps now he'd shut up and butt out. Louis swung his next pallet onto the pile with force. The ones underneath wobbled a bit but the pile stood firm. Josh didn't know what he was talking about. Pallets were *heavy*; they'd hold themselves in place.

By the time he'd thrown the last pallet onto his trailer, though, Louis wasn't quite so sure. The pile was still upright, but leaning. Naturally, Darren chose that moment to come over. Louis was bracing himself for a critical earful when the pile gave an ominous creak. It was falling.

"Darren!" Louis rushed at him and pushed. Darren fell forward onto his knees. A split second later, Louis saw a bright flash of light and was knocked off his feet.

Something had happened. Something bad. Everyone was gathered around Louis, staring down.

"What-?" His head felt strange and he couldn't work out why.

"You loaded the pallets unevenly," Josh said, and although there was criticism in voice, there was also worry.

Something like pain was gathering at Louis' temple. He touched a couple of fingers to it and they came away bloody. His mouth flooded with the taste of salt. Oh god – he was going to throw up. He twisted away from the others and spewed half-digested sandwiches onto the ground.

His workmates made various sounds of disgust and a few jumped back but Darren crouched down next to him. He had a wad of something soft in his hand and pressed it to Louis' temple. Louis recoiled, but Darren persisted.

"Compression," he said gently. "D'you think you can stand?"

" 'course I can stand."

But the task proved harder than Louis expected, and walking was worse. He couldn't seem to coordinate his feet. He wobbled, and swayed, and lost his balance.

Darren caught him, an arm about his waist. Louis giggled. Darren gave him a shake.

"Look at me," he said.

Louis looked. Darren was worried, really worried, his eyes boring into Louis'. It was weirdly intense and raised the hairs on the back of his neck.

"Wha' issit?" The question came out slurred.

Josh's face appeared behind Darren's. "You're looking for uneven pupils, right?"

Darren didn't answer. "Finish up here," he said. "I'm taking him to hospital."

Louis' head had started to hurt in earnest, plus he was utterly fed up. Hospitals were boring. Too much waiting about with nobody saying what was going on and too few handsome medics to provide distraction from pain. He took out his phone and checked his messages again. Still no reply from Bob. It would be just his luck if his text had got lost in the aether. He thumbed in another: word of the accident was bound to get back to Bob eventually and Louis didn't want him thinking he'd be too ill for their date. He'd just hit Send when a pimply bloke in a white coat appeared and led them to a consulting room.

He pulled an x-ray up onto a screen on the wall. It was like every other x-ray Louis had seen – ugly and grey. Darren, of course, found it fascinating.

"You were very wise to bring him in," the doctor told him, "but it's just a minor concussion. No sign of brain damage, and no bleeding. Take him home and keep an eye on him for the next forty-eight hours-"

"We are *not* together," Louis interrupted, appalled. "He's my boss."

"Oh." The doctor ran a finger around the inside of his collar. "Sorry. Do you have anyone at home? You shouldn't be on your own."

"My boyfriend's coming over tomorrow," Louis said, for the hell of it. It was worth it to see Darren's mouth twist in disgust.

"What about tonight?"

"My flatmate'll be in."

The doctor seemed satisfied with that. "Okay, well, get as much rest as you can. And if your head hurts, take paracetamol – not aspirin or antiinflammatories. And no alcohol. Can your flatmate come to take you home?"

"I'll do it," Darren said, before Louis could answer. "Uh, I mean, it's not like it's out of my way."

Regrowth

Louis hadn't slept more for than a few minutes all night: his head was thumping and his stomach had been invaded by hyperactive butterflies, tweaked out on the prospect of his evening with Bob. He popped out his morning dose of paracetamols and swigged them down with the water Em had put by his bed. Twenty minutes later, the thumping had dulled to a muffled thud but the butterflies were crazier still: in just nine hours, he'd be with Bob.

Em was already moving about, so Louis got out of bed and wandered downstairs to the kitchen where she was making coffee and toast.

"You look terrible," she said.

"Thanks." Louis helped himself to a piece of her toast in retaliation. "Just what a bloke with a red-hot date in his near future wants to hear."

Em frowned. "Seriously, you're still going to go? You're supposed to be resting, not participating in the sex Olympics."

"Exercise is good for you," Louis countered, stealing some coffee, too. "Everyone knows that."

"He's really that hot that you're prepared to risk giving yourself a stroke?"

"The whole point, Em, is that I get someone else to do that. And yes. He is. You wait 'til you see him."

"He's not the nutter who tried to kick our door in, is he?"

Louis half-choked. "Don't be ridiculous. That was Darren. I'm going out with Bob. Bob's like a real life version of Zac Efron. Darren's more like a bad-tempered version of a grizzly bear."

"Mmm, *bears*," Em said, and winked. Apparently, she still didn't believe he was done with men like Tom.

"Em, he doesn't like me," Louis said wearily. "And I don't like him."

Em didn't say anything. Just pursed her lips together and flicked through the morning paper for the crossword.

It really was only half-past six: Louis had checked on his phone, the kitchen clock and the telly. He was going to have to get through another half-hour with his heart in his throat and his innards fizzing. He paced the living room floor again, but it didn't help. He knelt on the armchair by the window and looked out into the street. The afternoon rain had turned to sleet and couple were walking past, arm in arm, under an umbrella. Meanwhile, Mr Davis was having the usual epic struggle reversing his Volvo up his drive. Louis wished Em were in. Her teasing might have distracted him from the niggling little voice at the back of his head which kept insisting Bob wasn't coming. He'd tried telling it to shut up, that there could be a million reasons Bob still hadn't texted him back, but there was no reasoning with it: it knew what it knew. Bob was far too successful and attractive to be interested in him; Louis hadn't had a proper date since Tom, just the odd fumble round the back of the Marquess of Queensberry; Louis wasn't bad-looking but there plenty who were better, and Louis was an idiot who couldn't handle the job ...

But, all of a sudden, it was seven o'clock.

He jumped off his chair. It wouldn't look good to be found staring forlornly out of the window like a dog awaiting its master. The trouble was, from the other side of the room, every passing car was potentially Bob pulling up, and Louis' hopes rose and plummeted so fast, he began to get giddy.

After thirty-five minutes, Louis had to face it: the voice in his head was right. Bob wasn't coming. He was being all noble, not wanting to take advantage when Louis wasn't one hundred percent. Louis snatched up the Iron Man cushion and hugged it to his chest.

Silly Bob. Louis was fine. Still a bit headachey, and not entirely steady on his feet, but fine. And besides, Bob's very presence would cure everything, right away.

Louis tossed the cushion aside with a sigh. He could text, he supposed - could even call - but if Bob was determined to be self-sacrificing, he doubted he'd be able to persuade him to change his mind. It was annoying, but it only made Louis like him more. Handsome, rich *and* selfless! If Louis wasn't careful, he'd fall in love.

He flicked on the telly. *Casualty* was about an accident at work. He promptly changed channels to *The X-Factor* on ITV. That was more like it! Pretty boys singing and dancing their hearts out. He should enter the show himself. It'd be better than another trip to the Jobcentre, the fate awaiting him when Darren got his way. Being paid zillions and taking his pick of sex-crazed groupies would suit Louis down to the ground. He decided to watch the show closely and take notes.

So, naturally, someone knocked at the door. Reflex irritation dissolved swiftly into hope. Perhaps Bob had merely been delayed. The ring-road was notoriously slow on Saturday nights. Louis sprang out of his chair and glanced out into the street for Bob's car. Bloody hell! Not only did he have a Jag but apparently an old-style Z4, as well. The man certainly had taste. Louis hurried to the door.

But it was Darren standing there, hands stuffed into his pockets, looking every shade of glum.

"He's not coming," he announced, before Louis could speak. "And no, there's nothing wrong. Other than his wife coming home early from New York."

"His wife?" Louis echoed, and even from his own mouth, the words sounded weird. Hollow. *Wrong.* Sometimes, the English language made no sense.

"Thought you should know," Darren said with a shrug. The sleet was heavier now, turning to snow.

Louis grasped desperately at this straw. "He could've got snowed in."

"His wife," Darren said slowly, watching Louis' face like he wanted to see each word land, "flew back yesterday. She was supposed to be out there 'til the end of next week."

Okay - the words were making a *kind* of sense now, in that Louis was following them, but grammar wasn't meaning. There was no logic in what Darren was saying.

"He can't have a wife," Louis said. "He asked me out. He's *gay*."

The snow was coaxing Darren's hair into dark, auburn curls. It looked almost pretty as he shook his head.

"No, he's *not*. I don't even reckon he's bi. He's just an arse. Likes playing with people's feelings. It's how he gets off."

"If he's such an arse, why did he send you to say he's not coming? Why not just leave me hanging?"

"He didn't send me. Josh phoned, wanting to know if you were okay. He just mentioned that Carol was back in passing."

Suddenly it all made sense: Darren was lying. Josh fancied Bob and Darren hated Louis. Together, they'd concocted this story because they each had their reasons for wanting rid of him.

"Josh 'just mentioned' it 'in passing'," Louis said, putting ice into his voice. "How would *Josh* know what Bob's 'wife' was doing?"

Darren blinked, slow and hard.

"He's her brother," he said softly. "Josh is Bob's brother-in-law."

It was the truth, Louis could tell, and some part of him was surprised at how little it hurt.

"Why the hell didn't you tell me that?" he demanded – no, *snarled*. He'd always fancied snarling. With his bone structure, he was sure it would look good on him. He'd liked to have snarled at Tom when he dumped him but was too busy ugly crying instead. Now, his time had come.

Darren had the grace to look awkward; he went a bit red. "Would you have believed me?"

Probably not, Louis had to concede, but that wasn't the point. "You still should have told me," he said.

Darren took a deep breath in and let a deep breath out.

"I thought I might not need to. I could see you were jealous whenever Bob talked to Josh. I thought if you thought his interest in him was ... romantic, rather than because they were family, you'd move on."

"You could have told me he had a *wife*! That would have done it."

"I know." Darren bit his lip. He had nice lips and Louis took a moment to appreciate them. "But I thought if I told you, you'd hate me."

"So what? You hated me."

"No. I thought you were a useless posh boy who'd be rubbish at the job - and I was right - but I never hated you."

The wind had picked up and changed direction, blowing snow into the house from the street. Bob's hair was getting thick with it again and wet snowflakes were frosting his stubble. He looked Louis straight in the eye ... and suddenly, Louis understood.

"*Oh.*" He smiled. Em was right: he always had liked bears. "You'd better come in."

"What?"

"You're going to freeze to death out there. Come on, get in." Louis stepped aside to let him pass. "Doesn't mean you're forgiven, or that this is going anywhere."

Darren slapped the worst of the snow from his coat and shook his head to dislodge it from his hair.

"And you'd better not have a secret wife." Louis wagged a warning finger as he shut the door.

Darren smiled. He had a really nice smile. And

he wasn't a *bear* bear like Tom. He was more of a ... What was the word? Oh yeah: otter. Darren was an otter; a bit big and hairy, but toned. Louis led the way into the living room, feeling rather pleased with himself.

"So, how long have you liked me?" he asked.

"From the start. Despite your stupid tool joke."

Louis sniffed. "I'd never have guessed."

"Well, you weren't paying attention, were you?" Darren said, his smile now a grin. "You were too busing checking out Elliot and everyone else who turned up. With all that distraction around, you couldn't see the, er, *wood* for the trees."

Wild

by Emmalynn Spark

My husband sat by the fire with his pipe, eyes closed. He looked the very image of contentment: fat and plush and rich. Old, too. Nearly twice as old as me. I was lucky to have him, people said.

I sat back from the fire. Close enough to be on hand should he need me, far enough to not draw attention. My sewing rested in my lap, my fingers working, making neat little stitches without my mind having to intervene. Much of my work went better when my mind didn't intervene. Wash, clean, cook, lie, spread.

A breeze blew through the room. My spine straightened. My husband opened one indolent eye. In the hearth, the fire quivered.

"The door," I said, redundantly. He grunted, didn't move. It would only be her, slipping in. There was no need to move, but suddenly my sewing felt heavy in my hands. The kitchen. I should go to the kitchen.

My husband's eyes were shut again, though he was still listening. I put my sewing down. Stood. He didn't say anything.

I closed the door behind me when I left the room. Then I dared to hurry. I knew he'd hear my steps, but I couldn't bring myself to care. My husband wouldn't say anything. The three months of our marriage had been built on his saying as little to me as possible and my saying as little as possible in general.

In the kitchen, the fire was low. My stepdaughter crouched over it, warming her hands.

When the old ladies had arranged my marriage, they'd talked about my stepdaughter. A girl only a few years younger than me,. she'd be a helpmeet. A companion. I wouldn't have to be alone in my marital home because she would be there with me. I wouldn't need to fear the woods so close at my door, worry about fairies stealing me away in the night. Not with a friend to walk with me. Not until she was married, anyway, by which point I would have been mistress of the house for almost a year. Not that I need fear for her leaving. She's been of marriageable age for six months now and the possibility of a suitor seems unlikely.

She looked at the door with wide eyes, body tensed to run, then relaxed when she saw it was me. She was wild. There were leaves and twigs caught in her red hair, which had been perfectly smooth when she'd slipped out that morning. The dress I'd carefully washed and ironed was now stained with mud and crumpled. Her shoes were gone and her bare feet had trekked black soil over my polished floor. She didn't look like a young lady primed for marriage, for family. She didn't look like anything I could define.

She smiled at me.

"Good evening," she said, polite as anything. "Would you like to come sit with me for a while?"

I shouldn't. I should run back out. Slip back into the living room and take up my sewing. Let the stitches numb me. Listen to my husband's snores until the time came to roll him to bed.

I took the chair from the corner of the kitchen and brought it to the fire. Sat down, watching her carefully. She smiled, open and unguarded, relaxed. She shifted so her filthy feet were held out to the fire. Her father would be livid about the loss of her shoes. He would rage and shout and she would laugh and go.

"How was the forest?"

She looked up, like she hadn't expected to hear me speak. I couldn't blame her, I hadn't expected it either.

"The forest?" she asked, smiling. "What do you think the forest's like?"

Dark. Cold. It was so close here, behind the house. It was almost at the bottom of our garden and sometimes, when I was outside, I could hear the whisper of the wind in the leaves.

My stepdaughter took a twig from her hair. She twirled it between her fingers and held it out for me. I took it. It felt like any other twig.

"The forest," she said, slowly, "is a place where there are no rules. When I'm in the forest, I can be anyone I want and there's nobody to stop me. In the forest, the best fruits grow all year, though you must always be careful never to gorge and to be thankful for what you take. In the forest, the moss cushions my feet and the trees hold me close. The flowers bow to me and the birds sing."

As she spoke, I felt myself swaying closer, caught in the magic of her words. Beautiful words. But I'd heard other things, whispered things.

"The fairies?"

She smiled a feral smile and I pulled back. She followed me, leaning over and resting her elbows on my knees, gazing up into my eyes. There was something about her that wasn't quite human, there in the firelight. I wondered if it was eating the fruit in the forest that did it.

"What do you know about the fairies?"

Nothing good.

I knew they took people. I knew that they would trick you, draw you in and then trap you. I knew that you might spend a day with them and come back to find a year had passed. I knew a fairy promise was worth less than the breath it took to say it.

"They aren't like you think," she said. She met my eyes and the firelight made her pupils dance. My legs burned where she touched me. I found myself leaning in closer. Wanting to catch every wisp of her breath.

"Tell me."

"They're cruel enough, yes," she said, so softly I had to lean in again to hear. Close enough that our foreheads nearly touched. "Like people. But they're wonderful too. To see them dance, it's a thing of beauty. To see them twirl. Their laughs are like bells. I watch them for hours. If only you could see." She was too wild. But, then, I supposed fairies might have strange tastes.

"I'd like to see but..."

"They're as wonderful as they are terrible. It's a strange thing, to know as you watch them that they could ruin you. To know that you only carry on in your life because they suffer you to. Because it makes them laugh. Their pet human. I couldn't imagine her as anyone's pet. It's not a free life, to live with the fairies, but it's interesting. "

"But it's so dangerous," I whispered. It was easier to talk, somehow, with our heads so close together. When the word need only be a breath. "Why go at all?"

My stepdaughter raised a hand. She touched my cheek and, though her manner was rough, her skin was smooth. I leant into it, not thinking. My eyes drifted closed and my heart ached. Such a soft, gentle touch. She slid her hand down to my neck, cupped my jaw. She leant closer. Our foreheads pressed together, then our cheeks, then our lips.

Everywhere she touched me, I was on fire. My hands reached for her, tangling in her ruined dress and creasing it more. She laughed against me and I felt something inside me loosen, something I hadn't known was wound tight. I laughed, too. Little and scared but real.

She moved, pushed her way onto my lap, and I shifted for her. Opened for her. It had never been this easy before. I ran my hands over her back. I crushed her to me.

She sighed and her eyelashes brushed my cheek. I had an absurd desire to crawl into her skin. To hide myself in her arms and never emerge again.

Then she pulled back and as she moved a simple tug at my sleeve made me follow her. Guided me to my feet and had me reaching for her, even as she danced away across the kitchen. Her eyes didn't leave mine as she reached the kitchen door, pushed it open.

The forest sat at the bottom of the garden. Dark. Cold. She skipped down the path, cast smiles back at me over her shoulder.

Behind me, the fire spluttered in the draught. It was nearly night. My husband would be waiting.

On the edge of the forest, my stepdaughter held out her hand.

I took off my shoes, and followed.

Razorback
by Megan Elizabeth Allen

They sent me into the woods with a bottle of antifungal meds and a small bag of supplies. Exile, they called it.

They probably should've killed me.

The straps of the pack dug into my shoulders, heavy with bottles of water, packets of food, and medical supplies Fia had pushed inside over my protests. I'd crossed the ravine into the state park a few hours after dawn, and as I approached the road to Lake Dunn the sun was high and the sky was the kind of endless blue that'd usually lift my spirits. Looking up at it, all I felt was loss like an opening pit in my chest. Hollow, thinking about the things I wouldn't see again. The people.

It was cooler under the trees. Oak and pine, mostly, leaves just starting to turn as the nights dipped toward freezing. I thought of sitting underneath one of the tallest, straightest trees and just giving up.

Shifting my pack, I stepped onto a trail I'd last walked with granddaddy. Without constant upkeep, leaves obscured the winding dirt path, and I might have lost my way if not for the familiar landmarks, a boulder that had split in two, a signal tree that grew oddly sideways before shooting up, the moldering trunk of an oak, wider than I was tall.

A breeze came off the wide, shallow creek that ran just east of the path, stirring the leaves and lifting sweaty strands of hair off my neck. This deep in the Ridge, the land was just a jagged series of hills sharp as knives, and the trail crossed them in a series of switchbacks and cut-throughs as I pushed deeper into the forest. Cresting a hill that overlooked the lake, I paused. I was probably a mile from Uncle Dave's place.

When everything happened, and I'd been trapped at granddaddy's house while the world ended, we'd thought about hiking up to Dave's trailer. Granddaddy had known Dave for about fifty years, and trusted him. Dave raised pit bulls as a hobby, and so lived in about as isolated an area you can get, on the edge of the state park, in a small trailer powered by generators, supplied with well water and a septic tank, surrounded by ten foot chain link fencing. The ideal place to ride out the apocalypse.

But granddaddy worried about trying to travel the earthquake damaged roads, and crossing a town he was sure had been overrun by zombies. I knew most of that worry had been for me.

Then he died, and all my other plans fell apart. Now here I was, back at the beginning. Headed to Dave's.

The air seemed thick almost, so that the sunlight lay in it, and dazzled my eyes. Beneath it the water of the lake was black and gleaming, and gold glinted off the small ripples kicked up by the light breeze. The sun was lower in the sky, limning some small blue clouds on the horizon. The woods were quiet, just the buzz of insects, crickets sawing in the heat, the occasional plop of a surfacing fish.

I flexed my hand in its tight bandage, and turned back to the path.

The surrounding woods started to feel real familiar. The ground leveled off a little, and the trees were mostly pine, straight and towering overhead, their needles carpeting the path and making the buzz of insects and soft chirping of songbirds seem muffled. There was less undergrowth, and I could see farther, to a point of light that marked the end of the trail. On aching legs, I trotted forward, suddenly excited to see Dave again. I hadn't come up here with granddaddy in a few years. Dave had visited with granddaddy after grandma died, checking in on him every few days so he wouldn't be too alone. But it had been a while since we'd make the hike up to see the dogs.

I broke out of the cover of the trees into the small meadow, out of breath, and saw the trailer, the high fence, the kennels, the red water tank. It was all there. Something in me relaxed, and I strode forward hesitantly. I'd have to let him know about granddaddy, which would be a blow. And what had happened to me. He'd take care of things if I did get infected, I was sure of it.

But when I reached the gate, it was open.

Keeping my bandaged hand close to my chest, I pushed the gate open with the other. It creaked loudly, and the constant brum of insects quieted for a moment before starting up again.

Nothing moved.

I dropped my pack to the dirt and pulled my favorite knife, the one granddaddy had given me for Christmas a few years back, with a carved wooden handle and saw teeth halfway up the blade. I had the gun in my pack, but something told me to keep this quiet.

Inside the fence, Dave's place was sadder and smaller than I remembered. The once-towering kennels only came to my shoulder; the yard was just dirt and trash and broken branches; even the trailer looked smaller, its sides filthy and oddly crumpled. The storm must've rolled through here, too, I thought.

"Dave?" I called out softly, willing my voice to

carry but not too far. "Uncle Dave, it's Maddie, um, Madison Singer." No response. "Um, Mike Delany's granddaughter?"

Still nothing. I edged forward, feeling nerves creep up my spine and shiver down my arms. "Dave, I'm coming in," I called out in warning, stepping toward the trailer.

There was a blur of movement to my left, a sound of fast-thumping feet, and a small body slammed into my knees.

I yelped as I went down, and it was on me: a small wriggling body frantic in my arms, short fur covered in dirt, tongue licking at my face.

Barely tossing my knife away in time, I got both hands on the puppy, laughing. "Hey there, hey, what're you doing?" I asked him, getting my hands on his strong, smooth shoulders but just for an instant, palming his neck, his sides, and he jumped about in my lap. "You must be one of Dave's." He was a pit bull, probably six months old and friendly as hell. "Where is everybody, huh? Where's Dave?"

He couldn't tell me, but he calmed down enough to sit back, panting through a wide-mouthed grin as I sat up. "You here all alone, buddy?" I asked him, levering myself upright and patting him on the head while he writhed joyfully at the attention. He was a good looking dog, a solid slate gray with a white blaze down his chest and startlingly blue eyes. I tousled his ears a little, and he panted an open mouthed grin. "Well, come on, then."

He stayed on my heels as I walked the rest of the property, following me into the small trailer – empty drawers suggested Dave had fled rather than died, and while there weren't a lot of supplies left, there was a bag of dry food in a cabinet near the sink. I shook it – half full. "I'm gonna have to track down some more food for you," I murmured, and the puppy wriggled to hear my voice.

I poured some kibble into a cereal bowl and left the puppy scrambling to get it down while I kept looking for clues.

There wasn't much else to see, though. A few cans of food, a bottle of cheap bourbon, a few flannel shirts.

I sank down into the only chair, cut through with a pang of sorrow. And self pity. The bite throbbed under its bandage, and I flexed my hand as if to spite it, almost pleased by the pain it caused.

The puppy put his chin on my knee, and whined.

Patting his head helped, and I dug up a smile for him. "Thanks, little guy," I whispered, rubbing his soft ears. Dave didn't dock his pits, and his ears flopped ridiculously about his square head as I tousled them. He just grinned up at me, and I had to laugh, a little spark of joy in the overwhelming pit of grief.

That night I secured the fence, and brought in my pack, before seeing to my hand.

Just looking at the bandage, I could almost hear Fia's voice ringing in my ears, just an echo of it, screaming as she went down.

I shook myself. It'd been worth it. Even if our theory was wrong, and this did kill me. It was worth it.

I scrubbed out the wound with fresh well water and Dave's harsh yellow soap, just like Fia had shown us, gritting my teeth and scouring the abraded flesh until I drew blood. The puppy whined at me from the other side of the bathroom door. I was panting with the pain of it, my hand shaking a little. After letting it bleed freely for a few minutes, I scrubbed it again, forcing myself to breathe.

Two more rounds of this, and I slapped on a thick paste of colloidal silver and topical antifungal cream Fia had put together, covered the bite itself with a square of sterile gauze, and wound an ace bandage around the whole thing. The puppy was still scratching at the door. I pushed it open with a toe. He forced himself through the crack, his small body vibrating as he pressed himself against me. My hand was trembling. The fingers wanted to curl in. I tried to force them straight, stopped, hissed at the pain. The puppy whined. I patted his head with my other hand. "It's okay, little guy," I whispered. Even I didn't believe me. "It's gonna be okay."

I woke reluctantly the next morning, hand aching like the puppy had been biting it all night, like it was trapped in those pit jaws. It was hard to get out of bed, even harder to think of a reason to bother getting out of bed. The national guard guy had said there was a seventy thirty chance, better if you were fit, and we had the antifungal cream and the oral meds. But he'd had all that, and he'd still been infected.

I didn't like those odds.

Dim sunlight filtered through the high windows and made patterns on the sheet I was curled under, a comma around the hot pain in my arm. Time passed, and I let it. The light moved. Hunger hollowed out my stomach, but there was something almost pleasing about that dull pain, a whisper next to the scream of the bite. I'd been so focused on surviving, on getting back to Memphis, on helping Fia find her sister, and now. And now.

The puppy leapt up on the bed, whining.

He was licking my face and my hands came up the shield it and suddenly a laugh bubbled up.

"You hungry, little guy?"

He jumped down, tail working furiously, and I followed him to the kitchen, moving about as slow as one of the zombies. The trailer had just a short hall between the bedroom and kitchen, but the puppy turned back to urge me on, then ran back to the kitchen, then back to me. I dished out some of the food, and he dived into it head first. I ate some stale cereal dry, and for a few minutes the trailer was filled with the sound of crunching. Dave had set up a little table across from the sink, beneath one of the few windows, and I sat there for a bit, watching the wind move through the trees, and thought.

There were only two options: I could live as if I were going to die, or I could die trying to live.

I stood up. The puppy barked, and I leaned down to pet his soft ears. "Wanna go fishing?" I asked his wide doggy grin.

After I scrubbed out the bite, and rewrapped my hand, I started poking around the various closets and outhouses within the high fence. Dave had two fishing poles stashed in the shed with a small tackle box. I filled a bag with the box, water, and a pistol, and opened the gate. A low whistle, and the puppy bounded over to follow.

The early morning sunlight had given way to a light rain, and we cut through the forest back toward Lake Dunn with the cool mist settling on us. It was dark beneath the tall loblolly pines, just a bit of gray light leaking through the close branches, and we moved almost soundlessly over the soft needles. The puppy bounded excitedly at first, running in circles around me to sniff everything he saw.

The mist felt good on my skin. After a few miles, the puppy wore himself out, and, tongue lolling, came neatly to heel. The land folded in strange cuts and ridges, and we had to cross one to get to the lake. The trees were smaller here, and more varied, patchy-barked toothache trees, beech and hickory, a few signal trees, their trunks moving in strange parabolas and abrupt angles.

The ground dropped precariously down into a gully. We slid down its side, my boots scrabbling for purchase in the damp leaf litter, the puppy scrambling enthusiastically after me. The bottom of the gully was covered in a dense growth of low-lying saplings and bushes, mostly paw paw, fruit hanging high and green, thin-twigged Black Walnut, branches drooping like the leaves of a fern, the ground hidden by dense sprays of May-apple. We were swallowed by the green, and couldn't see through it. I moved slowly around the delicate plants, ducking beneath fronds of paw paw leaves and stepping over clusters of glossy green Daphne. I heard a distant rustle, and stopped behind a tallow, its spade shaped leaves just shading a faint pink. The steady buzz of insects didn't falter or shift. The pup stopped with me, looking about in a curious fashion. Moving slowly, I stepped forward.

The other side of the ravine rose abruptly out of this abundance, so steep I had to move up in on all fours, pulling on thin saplings, my feet sliding in the thick loam.

The puppy bounded up easily, and waited at the top of the ravine, cocking his head side to side while he peered down at me, as if wondering why I was so slow to make the climb.

At the top, I had to pause.

It was the ridge overlooking the lake. We'd approached it from a different direction, and coming out of the tree cover I was suddenly standing in the sun looking at the bright water. A cool breeze had kicked up, and scattered the clouds, and I went down to the lakeshore with something approaching hope.

The forest ran right up to Lake Dunn. Flooded sometime after the war, the lake was once a deep, steep-sided valley, choked with dead trees, just a thin rim of dirt between you and drowning. There was a beach around the other end. I remembered grandma telling me they trucked in tons of sand to maintain a safe swimming area for the kids, but this side of the lake was in its own way dangerous. There was no gradual drop off, like at the beach, just a straight plunge to the bottom. The little bits of sun behind the scattered clouds sparkled off in the distance, but here beneath the overhanging trees was still and dark, the air close and wet. Logs ran out across the water, and sticks poked up out of it like thin, dead fingers.

Perfect for fishing.

Catfish would seek shelter among the logs and the caves carved into the sides of the ridge by the action of the water, and so that was where I cast my line. The puppy splashed at the edges of the water a bit, but came when called, and settled down next to me. I had one hand on the rod, and my bandaged hand on his softly heaving back. The damp loam slowly seeped into the both of us. It was a cool, damp afternoon, and I hooked a string of catfish before heading back.

Toward evening the clouds stretched and thinned and the sun slid behind them, casting half the sky an eerie, muted ochre that melted slowly into gold. The trees stood black against the sky, and it was harder to move among them, the forest cast in a deep gloom. The trailer in its clearing was like a beacon, dull silver shining even against the bright sky, and back within the fence before dark I felt a swallowing sense of fondness for the ragged place.

The puppy frisked about, whining, and I set out his bowl of kibble while I cleaned the fish, starting with a clean cut down the middle. Tossing the guts into the puppy's bowl, I cut just through the skin behind the gills, wedged the heads onto sharp sticks, and pulled the skin off in two broad pieces, like forcing off too-tight gloves. The pallid flesh gleamed oddly in the last of the evening light, jiggling as I cut it off the bone. The puppy put his head on my knee toward the end of this messy process, eyeing the stack of bones with pleading eyes, but, not wanting him to choke, I tossed the bones in a bucket on a high shelf to bury later. The filletsI tossed in cornmeal and fried in Canola oil over a small fire in the yard. People have other thoughts on this, but to my mind, there's nothing else you can do with catfish. Fried, the flesh becomes light and tender. Sautéed or baked or put in a stew, and catfish is a soggy, slimy thing.

Sitting before that fire with good, hot fish and a can of warm beer, I could almost imagine Fia sitting across from me, her teeth gleaming white against her dark skin in the flickering light, sharing a meal and cracking jokes to stave off the dark. But there was just me, and the puppy, who was still begging for fish.

I looked up at the sky, fully dark now, all that gold melted to a muddy black. I couldn't see any stars. My hand was hurting, and a pang went through my chest.

Just a few weeks, and I'd be with her again. Or dead.

The bite was still an angry red. I scrubbed it furiously, forcing the bristles deep into the flesh, soap foaming up like something rabid. When I'd finished, my hand was shaking, and wouldn't quite close into a fist. But the bite was red. Still red.

The forest became an odd sort of comfort. I couldn't stand to stay inside the fence for more than a few hours. The day I had to wash out the ace bandage and let it dry on a clothes line I about went out of my skin. I taught the pup to come to a particular whistle I'd used on grandma's sheep dogs – like a whippoorwill, two low and long, one high and short. That only took a few hours, so I taught him to stay, fetch, and carry, keeping both our minds off the boredom. But every other day, I was out in the trees.

I reacquainted myself with stretches of woods I hadn't walked in years, noting the smallest changes – where the trails had weathered with winter storms, newly fallen trees, shifts to the creeks and hills, rabbit runs and traces of whitetail deer. The woods don't stay the same from one day to the next, much less across the years, but they have a rhythm that you can learn.

The puppy woke me, whining, his tongue rough on my face. I fended him off weakly, moaned. My head felt hot, and I had that shivery feeling, like my bones weren't entirely happy in my skin. After feeding the dog, I climbed back into bed.

I dreamed of before, of a holiday meal with family, in grandma's kitchen. Everyone alive and together, like we hadn't been in years. In the dream, grandma hugged me, held me close. She was wearing her favorite red sweater, and she whispered in my ear that she loved me.

Tears had dampened my pillow when I finally thrashed awake. I thought of the last nightmare I'd had, and Fia's arms around me, and felt even more alone.

That afternoon I went back to where I'd seen a few sassafras saplings and gathered a few roots. They made a deep red tea, faintly sweet, that I sipped on, constantly, through the rest of that day and into the night, until the fever cooled and, in the early hours of the morning, finally broke.

The wound was still red. But I thought it might

be healing.

I came upon a place where the creek widened out, just a shallow bit of water running over smooth brown pebbles, and the trees hung down over the clear water so that it looked like that creek in *Tombstone*, the one where Wyatt walked out in the middle of a gunfight, as if untouchable, to shoot the evil Clampett guy. Just like that creek.

I wanted to tell Fia about it. I wanted to tell Fia about everything.

Through the trees there was a flood of light, like a meadow where I didn't remember a meadow. Out of deep shadow rose the light-drenched corpses of trees, so buried in kudzu they were just vague shapes, just impressions of trees. It was probably October, I thought, and smirked: trees wearing ghost costumes. I didn't enter the clearing. Anything could be lurking beneath the waist-deep vines. There's something inherently eerie about the barren spaces created by kudzu. A strange beauty to them, too, shafts of light dancing on glossy green leaves, but in spite of the green they were places of death.

Even this, Fia might find interesting.

After the fourth day after the fever, wound still red, the edges somewhat glossy with healing, I wondered if they'd left for Memphis yet. If they would leave for Memphis at all. Jenny had no reason to go, and was only going to follow me there because I'd guilted her into it. Alejandro wanted to go to Little Rock, where his grandma was; he'd only agreed on Memphis because Fia and I both had family there, and he'd felt like he owed me. But Jenny might decide to stay, or Alex might go west instead of east, and Fia might already be on the road. We'd decided on three weeks, three weeks to be sure I wouldn't turn and kill us all. I was counting the days until I could return. But what if something happened? What if they left without me?

In the midst of these fears, the woods provided a distraction. In the mornings I went out early enough to watch herds of deer grazing in the meadows, white tails flicking anxiously. A noise, and they would bound away as one, tails up like flags. There was an abandoned hunter's stand near one of these meadows, and I brought a thermos of coffee and breakfast there a few times.

As the sun rose, the deer would creep out of the mist that rose off the trees, and spread unevenly over the meadow, some hanging nearer the edge, one investigating the small forester's hut, a few always on watch, ears turning and heads up. A rabbit hopped out to join them, small and timid in its movements. I watched, enthralled, thinking of Bambi and Thumper.

In a movement too quick to follow, one of the stags darted its head out and clamped his mouth around the rabbit. In a second it was over, the rabbit swallowed down. I could only stare. Queasiness roiled though my gut.

I decided not to return to the hunter's stand.

The sunset painted the sky a shade of pale peach behind the black fringe of the pine branches, little black needles.

I stood at the lip of the hollow, staring down into the rushing water. I had the strangest feeling that if I just leaned forward, and let myself fall, I would keep falling, through the swirling water, through the vortex, into some other world.

The puppy barked. I blinked, and straightened up.

I was walking near the creek, three fish on my string, coming up a hill and there was a sound somewhere behind me, a rustling, and odd grunting. I turned to look.

"Oh god," I breathed.

A wild boar. A razorback. Not forty yards away, and there was something about it that didn't look right in ways that sent terror shivering up my spine. It screamed, high pitched and awful. Raised the hairs on the back of my neck, sent gooseflesh crawling up my arms.

I dropped the fish and ran.

There was noise behind me, hooves in the leaves and that awful grunting. Trees whipped by. My boots were slipping in the thick leaf litter. I could just hear it running over the thundering of my heart.

Then I remembered. The deer stand.

I veered toward the meadow, legs stretching out now that I had a destination. Splashed through the creek, bounded up the bank using tree trunks like hand rails, running again. There was splashing behind me. A squeal. I spotted the stand, hit the tree at a full sprint and hauled myself up the side faster than I thought possible. Flung open the tarp and--

"Holy shit!" a man yelled, and he was holding a rifle, there was a kid next to him and I was clinging to the edge of the deer stand with a wild fucking boar at my back.

"It's coming, let me in!"

"Are you infected?" he yelled back, rifle wavering.

"No, fuck, let me in!"

He lowered the gun and I dived onto the boards just as the boar slammed itself into the base of the tree.

"What the fuck is that?"

Another blow. The whole tree shuddered.

"A boar," I panted. "I think it's infected."

"No shit," he snapped. The walls of the little

stand were shaking with each blow, and we stared at them. After a moment, it got still.

I looked over at the man. He was huddled in his corner, hugging the rifle. He was about my age, maybe a couple of years older. The kid, no more than eight, looked like he was in shock, clinging to the man's leg and pale, so pale.

I pulled myself up and poked a head out. The boar was just below us. It stood, very still, its sides moving gently but not as if it was breathing. It looked like a boar, mostly, but there was something about the shape that seemed wrong. Off.

"I ain't seen other infected animals," the man said quietly.

"Pigs and humans are real similar," I whispered, still staring at the boar. "Diseases cross over all the time."

"Shit," he muttered. "What's it doing?"

"Just standing there." It wasn't still, exactly. Sort of wavering on its feet in a very small circle, a constant juddering beneath its hide.

"What, uh, what should we do?"

"Kill it," I said firmly, pulling out my pistol. "This won't make a dent. You any good with that rifle?"

He hugged the rifle closer. "No, uh, haven't needed it yet."

I turned to look at them. "What are y'all doing out here, anyway?"

He looked shifty, and said, "Trying to get to some kin over near Jonesboro."

"Uh huh. The kid okay?" The kid did not look okay, pale and sweaty even in the cold air.

He looked down, nodded.

"Well, fuck. Where's he bit?"

"He's not ..." The gun wavered.

"Hey, woah, I'm not judging. I was bitten a couple of weeks ago. You taking care of him?"

His eyes lit with a sudden hope. "You were bitten?"

"Yeah," I said, flashing my bandaged wrist. "It's healing right up."

"So he might not get infected?"

"Well, um. How long ago was it? And what are you treating it with?"

He shook his head. "A couple of days ago, just before we ended up in this stupid park. And, uh, we didn't have much. Soap and water. But he might be okay," he said, a little desperately. "Yours healed."

"He'll need medicine." I thought for a moment. "You should come back to my place after we kill this damn pig."

"You have meds?"

"Yeah, antibiotics, steroids, and antifungals."

I might still need them myself, but I figured I could share. I knew where to get more, after all.

"Thank you, that's ..." The man seemed unable to keep speaking, his throat closing up.

"I'm Maddie," I offered. "What's your name?"

"Jon, uh, Jonathan. This is Tag."

"Tag?" I smiled. "That's a real cute name."

"Thanks," Jonathan managed, sniffing.

There was a rustling from below. I grimaced. "Can I borrow your rifle?"

"Have at it," he said, passing it over.

The rifle was fairly light in my hands, lever-action with rich wood at the stock and barrel. "How many rounds in there?"

"It's fully loaded," he said, sounding slightly offended. "Six, plus one in the chamber."

"Wonder you didn't blow your head off," I muttered, double checking the chamber and sighting down at the boar, "keeping a round chambered like that."

It was still wavering, and I ignored the man's

indignant "Hey!" as it shuffled in place.

There was something off about the shape of its head. From up in the hunter's stand, the boar was no more than ten feet away, yet I couldn't make out any firm details. Like it was behind a film, or in a fog. I squinted, pulled back to check the rifle's open sights. Cleaned off my glasses. Looked at the boar again.

"What's wrong?" Jonathan asked.

"Nothing," I murmured absently, pushing the rifle into my shoulders. "Just having a little trouble seeing the damn thing."

"What the hell is that supposed to mean?"

"Its head, there's a ... fuzz around it. Or something." I sighed. "Just, cover your ears," I said, and fired.

The first cartridge plowed through the top of its head. A strange, black liquid, thicker than blood, splattered across the leaves. But the boar was still on its feet, and now it knew where I was.

It rammed the base of the tree again, rocking the whole tree. I grabbed the edge, nearly dropping the rifle.

"Hang on," Jonathan yelled, grabbing Tag around the shoulders.

"I think I just made it mad."

There was a high squeal, and another thud. The tree shook, showering the forest floor with leaves and gumballs.

"Shoot it again," Jonathan demanded.

I poked my head over the edge of the stand, and lying on my belly tried to get the rifle pointed down at the boar. Another thud, the tree swaying now, and I had to pull back.

"I can't get an angle on it," I said, frustrated. "Not while it's right below us."

Jonathan edged forward. "Lean out, I'll hold you."

I hesitated.

"I promise, I won't drop you," he said. "I'm stronger than I look."

"Alright, grab my belt."

He braced himself with a hand on my belt, his elbow hooked around a branch, and with the extra support I leaned out into space.

I waited through another attack, and the tree felt unsteady, now, swaying even when the boar backed up for another charge. I sighted on it, fired, fired again. At this distance both shots hit home, but it still wouldn't go down.

"Are you even hitting it?" Jonathan said, his voice sounding strained.

I leaned out a little further, and snapped, "Yes, three times."

"Well, that leaves four bullets, so maybe try something else."

I pulled back into the stand at looked at him. "Are you telling me you only had seven cartridges for this thing ... total?"

He glanced away shiftily. "It wasn't my gun, okay, I found it."

"Oh my god." I leaned back out, and he hastily grabbed my belt again. "We're not done talking about this." I shot the boar again, and it roared at me. "Damn it."

"That's three left."

"I know!" I fell back into the stand. "What else can we do?"

"Shoot it more?"

"The definition of insanity is doing the same thing and expecting a different result."

"So what, then? What else can we do?"

"I need a different angle," I said slowly, looking at nearby trees.

"No," he said, shaking his head. "You can't just

leave us in here."

"I've got three shots left before we're down to a fucking nine mil," I said. "We're out of options. Unless you have a forty five you failed to mention?"

"No," he admitted. "But what if you fall?"

"I won't fall," I said, edging closer to the hide's opening. "Just stay here, and try to keep its attention on you." I paused. "Shoot it a few times," I said, handing him my pistol.

"Right," he muttered. "Distract it."

The closest tree had a branch, fairly horizontal, not three feet away. I jumped for it.

And hit, hard, slamming into the wood. The branch swayed, and I wrapped all my limbs around it, clinging.

"You okay?" Jonathan asked.

"Yeah," I said shakily, "I'm good."

The zombified boar below us was still attacking the tree I'd just left, and as I slowly sat up, I felt cautiously optimistic that I'd gotten away with it.

The best way to shoot a pig in the brain is to shoot it through the ear, and I still didn't have a good angle on it.

Scooting along the branch to the trunk of the tree, I pulled myself up and moved around the trunk to another branch. The trees in this part of the woods were close enough that I could Tarzan my way out of this, probably.

It was easier getting into the next tree, a dogwood that grew slantwise and was like walking a highway compared to the sweet gum tree. That lead me to an oak, and I paused there, braced against its trunk.

With most of the leaves down, I had a good view of the boar. It was still charging the tree, the semi-regular thuds a little muffled now.

From this angle, I could see the outline of its

skull, and what was there, or wasn't there, made me shudder. The skull had deformed, as if pushed aside, and growths burst forth from within. As far as I could tell, the boar didn't have eyes anymore, or much of a face, just a bulbous, earthy mass. Filaments sprouted forth from it, surrounding the skull in a gray-ish cloud.

I couldn't understand how it was still standing, much less tracking us and attacking our tree.

It charged the tree again, then, ramming into the base so hard that a cloud of the filaments puffed up around its head. Disgust crawled through me, and I fired, putting two bullets in its ear.

It didn't fall. For a long moment it stood there, still fixated on the sweet gum's trunk. It swayed a little. I thought about my last bullet. There was movement from the stand, Jonathan leaning out. The boar swayed again.

"What are you waiting for?" Jonathan yelled. "Shoot it again!"

I adjusted the rifle a little, hesitating. Half a minute had passed, maybe a little more.

Then, all of a sudden, with an odd sigh, the boar fell over, twitched once, and was still.

"Is it dead?" Jonathan asked.

I stared down at it. "I don't know."

Dead things have a particular lack of movement about them, I'd been finding lately. We waited ten minutes or so; when the boar didn't move again, I climbed down from the tree and poked it with a stick.

It still didn't move.

"I think it's okay," I called up to Jonathan. "You can probably come down."

"Probably?" he objected, but was climbing down anyway, moving slowly to help the boy climb down with him.

Tag was shaking, just a little. "Come on," I said, passing Jonathan the rifle. "We should get back to my place."

I held my hand out for the pistol I'd given him.

There was a moment when he didn't move, just a moment. But then he handed it over, and I tucked it back in my belt.

Jonathan was paying a little more attention to the boar. "It looks funny," he said, picking up a stick of his own and poking at it. After a few pokes, he said, "What's this?" in rather a different tone of voice.

Something had caught on his stick, and came with it as he pulled it back, a clear strand attached to the boar's mouth by a hook that winked silver in the light.

"My fishing line," I said, remembering the string of fish I'd dropped. "I guess he ate my fish."

"Probably saved your life," Jonathan said, dropping the stick and the line with it.

"Probably," I said, unsettled. I looked up to the sky, which was bleaching of color as the sun sank toward the horizon. It was still bright, but wouldn't be for more than another hour or so. "Come on," I said, turning to the boys. "We should get back to my place."

With an hour of daylight left I was able to take them back to the trailer by a roundabout path they'd be unable to follow on their own. Tag got paler with every step, and at the bottom of the last hill Jonathan swept him up in his arms and carried him the rest of the way.

"How old is he?" I asked. That was a question to ask about kids, I figured.

"Oh, I don't know," Jonathan panted.

I stopped. "What?"

"He's not my kid," Jonathan said, shrugging a little.

"So what, uh, what are you doing with him?"

Jonathan was silent for a few steps. "We were with a group, a large group. We split off from one of the evacuation centers, after. Uh. Tag was, well, his parents didn't."

I nodded, looking down. "Yeah." We walked silently for a few steps. "So you're looking after him? That's really something."

"Least I could do," Jonathan said, voice a little dull.

"No, you could have done a lot less."

"Yeah, well."

"Come on," I said. "The trailer's just ahead."

The puppy rushed to meet us at the gate, and Tag perked up a little, distracted by petting the excited, dancing creature while I secured the gate. Jonathan watched them playing, an abstracted look on his face.

"I hate to break this up," I said to him quietly, "but we need to look at Tag's wound."

"Yeah," he said roughly, and went to round up the boy.

He came, silently. I'd never seen a kid leave a puppy that willingly, but I'd also not spent a lot of time around kids.

I set up a lamp, pulled out my med kit, and started some water boiling on the fire. I had some clean water in jars, and I used some of that to soak Tag's bandage. The blood had dried it stiff, and he whimpered as I worked at the cotton. "Sorry, kid," I said softly. Jonathan glanced at me, and I said, "You might have to hold him."

"What?"

"I'm going to have to scrub out the bite. It's called debridement. Getting rid of dead tissue. And it's gonna hurt like hell."

He paled, but nodded.

The bandage came off with a wet, soppy sound. I winced.

The shoulder had a chunk missing, and the wound was brown at the center, with red creeping up and down Tag's arm like streaks of paint.

"It's infected," I said, reaching for a bar of soap.

"Shit," Jonathan said.

He caught Tag around the shoulders, and I grabbed Tag's wrist, and scrubbed at the wound until fresh blood flowed, and then scrubbed a little more. Tag howled the whole time, and the puppy started to howl with him in sympathy, and the sound tore at my heart. But it had to be done.

The blood flow slowed. I patted the bite with a scrap of clean cloth, and peered down at it. There was something off about it, and I looked under the rim of my glasses.

"Oh my god."

There were silver filaments, fine as baby hairs, running through the exposed muscle. I shifted the lamp, and the threads glimmered in the light. My stomach turned.

"What is that?" Jonathan said, sounding disgusted.

"The fungus," I said. "It must be."

"What does this mean? What do we do?"

"I don't think there's anything we can do." I dropped Tag's arm, and the boy didn't move. He just stared.

"No," Jonathan said, "no, that can't be it. I, that's."

"I'm sorry."

He shook his head, like that deer shaking down a rabbit. "No, we can still try, you said there was medicine."

"Yeah, we can try." I fumbled through the bag until I found an unopened bottle of the antifungal pills. My hand was shaking, the pills rattling against the plastic, and I passed the bottle to Jonathan. "Get him to take one of those."

"Okay, yeah," he said nervously, shaking out one of the small pills. "C'mon, buddy," he said, reaching toward Tag.

The boy bit him in the hand, hard.

I gasped, jumping back. Jonathan howled, yanking at his hand, but Tag's teeth were set and he wasn't letting go. His eyes, filmy and white, rolled wildly as Jonathan shook him. The puppy was barking.

"Maddie," Jonathan yelled, "do something!"

I had my gun. My hands were still shaking. Tag let go and tried to bite again, and Jonathan yanked his hand back. "Shoot it!"

Tag crept forward, mouth gaping. I pulled the trigger.

The little body fell to the floor. Even with the shake in my hands, I couldn't miss at that distance. His brains splattered across the table and wall. I felt sick.

"Jesus," Jonathan said, panting. "He just, he."

The puppy nosed toward the body, and I pulled him back by the scruff of the neck. "We, uh, we have to wash that bite."

Jonathan looked down at his hand. "Jeez, yeah." He shook his head. "That poor fucking kid."

I pulled the puppy into the kitchen and shut him in. Jonathan was already dabbing at his hand. I grabbed it and starting scrubbing with the soap. He grit his teeth, not making a sound. He didn't look down at what I was doing, but over at the boy's body, the whole time, not taking his eyes off it. From the kitchen, the puppy's steady whining was the only sound.

I was wrapping a bandage around his hand when he said, "Can we bury him?"

I sat back. "Yeah, I guess. We should."

"Yeah," he echoed, shaking out his hand.

We dug a little grave near the fence, away from the well. Jonathan carried the little body out of the trailer, and laid him down in it so gently.

"What was his last name?" I asked, thinking we should make a marker, or headstone.

Jonathan shrugged. "I don't know. I don't even know his first name."

"So it isn't Tag?"

He laughed a little. "He, uh, he never said anything, never spoke, not the whole time I knew him. I guess he was traumatized, or something. After we got separated from our group, I had to call him something. He was my little tagalong. Tag for short."

There were tears in his eyes. I didn't mention it, just focused on filling in the grave.

"Guess I'll be joining him soon enough," he said bitterly, looking down at his bandaged hand.

"Maybe," I admitted. "But maybe not. We can do the same as we were planning, give you the rest of these meds. Scrub out the wound every day."

"How long until I know?"

"A couple of weeks, I think, to be safe." I looked down at the grave. "I can come check on you."

"You can't stay?"

I shrugged. "It's time I get back to my group."

"Right." He looked lost.

"You can stay here. I've been fishing, mostly, so there's still a lot of canned food, and there should be enough of the medication to see you through."

The last shovel-full of dirt pattered down on the grave with a sound like rain. "Yeah, fine," he said. "If I turn ..."

"I could leave you my gun, if, um, you think you'd want to, well, take care of it yourself."

"What about you?"

"This is America," I shrugged. "I can always find another gun."

"Well, thanks." He took the gun, thought for a second. "I guess."

I left that night. I didn't want to spend another night in that trailer, with Tag's brains still all over the wall. It was bad enough leaving Jonathan to face it, but I packed my things, took the puppy, and spent the night in the woods in a hammock twenty feet up an oak tree.

I set out at dawn the next morning, retracing my path back to the barn. We took it slow. The puppy had a little trouble keeping up, a combination of short legs and a short attention span. Even so, by mid afternoon we came over the last hill, and saw the barn just across the highway. Both horses were out in the paddock, and Fia, Jenny and Alex were sitting around a small fire, cooking.

They were all okay. The worry I'd been carrying with me for three weeks loosened its hold, and I started down the hill.

Alex saw me coming, and they all jumped up. My steps quickened a little. The puppy picked up on my excitement, and we ran the last little ways. Fia broke out in front of the others, running too.

We met in the middle of the highway. I dropped my bag, and the puppy danced around our feet. Fia caught me in a hug. I hugged her back, hard, feeling the familiar lines of her back beneath my hands. She pulled back for a moment, looked at me, and then kissed me.

Her lips were soft, and I melted against her.

She pulled back after a moment. "I thought I'd lost you."

I didn't know what to say, so I kissed her again.

"And who's this?" Jenny asked, and I looked over. She'd knelt beside the puppy and was tousling his ears.

I looked at the puppy for a moment. "That's my little tagalong," I said slowly, my arm slung around Fia's waist. "Tag, for short."

Land of Make Believe
by K J Lowe

Claire's blue canvas pumps slapped on the pavement as she marched away, fists clenched, arms swinging. Her ponytail bounced against the back of her neck, sweat prickling. The heat had turned the smooth black tarmac sticky, and it caught at the soles of her shoes with each stride. Heat haze blurred the path in front, and the estate was silent; everyone had retreated indoors away from the midday sun, cars and gardening abandoned, washing hung limply on the lines. Even the birds had been smart enough to seek shelter.

The hot air felt suffocating as she took gulping breaths. She wasn't upset, she wasn't crying, despite what they said. She was angry, yeah, angry. Stupid David Williams, stupid boys. As if she couldn't play their stupid, stupid game. They needed a girl if they were going to have the full superhero team, and it was too her favourite series. She clearly liked it better than them. David Williams didn't even remember all the episodes correctly.

Well, screw you, David Williams. She bit back a vicious grin, glancing to check no adults could see her think the forbidden phrase. Bet he didn't know that swear word. She'd got it from an American detective show she'd seen when she'd been allowed to stay up late, an illicit phrase she'd tucked away for the right occasion. Screw you all, she thought with even more satisfaction, as she headed out the other side of the new estate. Through the little passage between the houses, towards the hill and the copse.

The dirt path leading up the hill had become so parched, it had turned into crazy paving. She paused to scuff at the entrance to an ant nest but her heart wasn't in it, so she kept moving. Occasional grasshoppers chirped, or were they crickets? She wasn't sure what was the difference. She resolved to look it up at the library that weekend.

The air wasn't much cooler as she climbed higher; there were no trees on the side of the hill to offer any shade, just the sun continuing to beat down from a bright blue sky. She reached the crest and bent over to catch her breath. From here she could survey the uniform houses stretched out below. Her gran had said that it used to be farmland down there, but the new estate had gone up well before Claire was old enough to remember.

She sat down on the hard ground with a huff. The short grass scratched at her bare legs. She shifted her shorts out of her backside. They were a bit too short, like mum had said. Not that she'd ever admit that, with their frayed edges, they were too cool to stop wearing.

She pushed her sock down her ankle to check on her tan line. Not bad. It wouldn't be enough though, she supposed. Not stuck round here for the whole summer. Some people went abroad, Spain even. Her nan had tacky souvenirs on her mantelpiece from Costa del Sol, from when Mum was younger than she was now. God, even her Nan had been to Spain. It wasn't fair.

Jenny Brown had been to Spain, but she was a cow. Last year she'd spent the whole of the first morning back at school shoving her brown arm next to Claire's pale one; and Claire had been so sure she'd a good watch mark until then. Everyone had laughed with Jenny, even though some of them hadn't got a tan either. Everyone had ignored Claire's cool new pencil tin because of it. It wasn't fair.

Claire brought her knee up and began to pick at her last remaining scabs. She'd fallen in the playground on the last day of school. It'd bled loads and she'd basked in the temporary coolness such a dramatic injury had given her. Then the dinner-lady with the stiff ginger hair and stern face, who always wore thick tights and a wool skirt no matter the weather, had dragged her off to have it cleaned with a steri-wipe. Claire usually avoided her as she scared her, but she'd been surprisingly kind that day. She'd looked at Claire like she could see right inside her head. Then sighed about too many big thoughts making you trip over your own feet. Which hadn't made that much sense to Claire: you can't trip over *thoughts*, that's just silly.

A bark made Claire look up. In the distance, a woman was walking her dog across the hill. One of those dogs off the telly, the guide dog ones. Claire watched them listlessly until they disappeared down over the edge. Alone and quiet again. That was fine. She liked it like that. People ruined everything.

A chorus of high pitched peeps sounded faintly above her. She looked up and squinted at the flat blue sky. There. Swifts flying way up in the sky, barely more than black dots. Apparently, they never landed.

She wondered how much cooler it was up there, and if they were as high as a plane going on holiday. She lay back and watched them until her eyes went funny. She imagined very few people were smart enough to look up and notice the swifts. She liked to think they were a little private show, just for her.

She watched them drift away, taking their distinctive calls with them. Silence again, and a faint wisp of a cloud drifted by. Probably Cirrus. She nodded to herself. Stratus, Cumulonimbus, she loved how the names of clouds felt in her mouth. She'd memorised them all from Mum's big Philip's book.

A faint rustle behind her. She tipped her head back. There was a slight breeze tickling the tops of the leaves of The Wood on the hill, even though there was no hint of it on the ground. The Wood was out of bounds. Mum said she wasn't allowed to walk through it. None of them were, but they'd all been in as far as the big fallen trunk on double dares.

She should have been running around with a gang of friends right now. That's what was supposed to happen in the summer holidays, right? Adventures and playing out together, but whenever she went round to her friends' houses, there never seemed to be anyone in, even though she thought she could hear their mums inside. A couple of times, she'd carried on pushing the doorbell or knocking until she felt too embarrassed to stay any longer; she thought she could feel the neighbours watching her from behind the net curtains. No-one ever came round to knock for her either. She was bored. Not that she cared. She could play much better games on her own.

The rustle from The Wood again. Maybe it would be cooler in there. Her head was getting too hot to touch. She'd just go in a little, enough to let her head cool down. No-one would know.

The dappled shade was an immediate relief. She could stop squinting all the time. The grass was patchier, more hard dirt showing through and a few crunchy leaves on the ground, even in Summer. She hopped up onto the big fallen trunk. It wasn't that far in really, just enough to feel you were properly inside The Wood. It had been hollowed out but was still more than thick enough to take the weight of several kids jumping on it. Moss and some frilly mushrooms grew on the side of it. She had often wondered where it had come from. It seemed far too big to have been part of The Wood. The other kids had looked at her blankly when she'd tried to explain, but it seemed clear as day to her that it had to have been dragged here. If you stood it upright it would have been way taller than the other trees. It always looked like something had smashed it over, leaving the ends jagged and broken. It just didn't fit.

She sighed as she dropped down and straddled it. This was boring, she was boring, everything was just boring. Maybe though...

She knew she shouldn't. Her mum would be mad at her. Some of the older kids had said they'd been right to the middle of The Wood and met a weirdo. Really though, they were probably lying, and besides, what was going to happen in the middle of the day? She could go in just a bit further. Not that there was much point. No one would believe her if she told them she'd done it. A few more steps would be okay. It was much nicer in here. The sweat on her neck was getting cool. And her head didn't feel like it was being squeezed by the sun any more.

A pigeon, one of the big, dumb, stupid ones, cooed up in a tree. Just a little further. Hopping down, she picked up a stick and gave it an experimental swing. Maybe she'd take this, just in case. She made a few lunges forward with her sword stick. She could fight baddies with this, yeah. An adventure, a secret one. All the others would joke about going in, but she was going to be the one to find out what it was really like in the wood. And she wouldn't tell them, ha.

The ground got crunchier as she walked further in, dried out dead leaves and twigs. Hidden stones to trip her if she wasn't careful. It wasn't particularly dark, or even slightly scary. The light shone down through the trees still, but it was amazing how all the outside sounds just dropped away, how quiet it got. A squirrel hopped across the path in front of her, pausing suddenly when it spotted her, nose twitching. Rats with bushy tails, her dad called them, usually when one had chewed through the bird feeder again and run off with all the peanuts. Her dad had an ongoing feud with them now. The latest attempt to make them squirrel-proof had resulted in the squirrel just running off with the entire feeder instead. She couldn't help feeling he was losing the battle.

The squirrel ran halfway up a tree and stayed there flashing its tail at her as she walked past. She sided more with her dad to be honest. Everyone always acted like they were cute, but she found something off about their faces, something shifty, like they'd turn on you if you weren't careful. It chittered a warning at her and she stuck her tongue out at it.

She scuffed her feet along the ground, the layer of leaves getting deeper as she went. She dragged the stick against the tree trunks, but it was too thin to make any satisfying noises. Her foot hit a particularly big stone and she stopped to fish it out from under the debris. It almost filled her palm, smooth yet knobbly, with a few pock marks. It had a hole right through, just a bit too small for her to get the tip of her little finger in but big enough she could peer through it. She wondered where it had come from. She tucked it into her pocket, a treasure from her adventure.

The path, such as it was, weaved around the trees. It wasn't very interesting. She wondered about making a den or something, but there weren't that many other sticks lying around. She dug at the leaves and mud with her sword stick. Maybe there cool things hidden under the mud. It was a bit damper here, amongst the trees. She tried digging a bit with her stick, which promptly snapped. Oh great, typical. She threw it away. Boring. She contemplated turning back, but wouldn't it be cooler to say she'd walked all the way through?

Swinging herself one handed round a tree trunk, she found her eye caught by a splash of colour. Bright red mushrooms with white spots were scattered round the bottom. Wow, she'd never seen one of these outside a book before. They were dangerous to eat, she knew. She didn't touch it though. Everyone knew you'd die if you touched poisonous mushrooms. It was a shame. That would have been a fabulous treasure to bring back with her.

She strode on, humming random songs from the Top 40, and daydreaming dances to go along with them. Until she noticed that the light was dropping. The trees had become much thicker, cutting down the sunlight filtering through the leaves. The trees looked different, too. Not the familiar oak and sycamore, these were more like pine trees, more like the old trunk. They rose much higher and it was hard to see the tops.

She turned around, frowning. When had it all changed? The path she'd come down was now squeezed straight and tight between more towering trunks. Not the same one she'd been stumbling along. She scuffed her feet in fallen pine needles. These were like the trees she'd seen on holiday, not what they got round here.

There were more of those mushrooms and other plants as well. A bush of what looked a bit like big fuzzy dandelion heads. She reached out and brushed it lightly. The little umbrella seeds took off in a frightened flurry, twisting round each other up into the canopy. She stared open mouthed. There were harebells, snapdragons, and pretty, yellow trumpeted flowers all along the path. So many colours. Everything seemed softer in the fuzzy light. She crouched down and lifted one of the unfamiliar yellow flowerheads; and threw herself backwards with a yelp as it tossed its head roughly out of her grip. A chittering came from above, almost like laughter, but it was just another squirrel. It watched her for a moment then leaped off through the trees.

She stood up and brushed off her backside, slightly embarrassed. Right, nothing to see here. Just her imagination getting away from her. She eyed the yellow flowers suspiciously. Best leave them alone, just in case.

She absolutely didn't see their heads turning to watch her leave.

Obviously, she'd got a bit lost. Not sure how in such a small wood, but no worries, if she kept straight on, she'd come through eventually, right? She bit her lip and toed some bluebells. They tinkled gently. Nope, not listening, this is silly, she told herself. Keep walking.

The ground turned into a soft mat of not-quite moss, dotted with yellow daisy-like flowers, that smelled sweet as she walked on them. She bounced slightly on her heels. The ground was springy too. Green and red moss now grew on the tree trunks and old stumps. It looked like something from a fairytale book. The old one, with the colour 'plates'. Another chirruping noise came from the trees, and she caught another flash of colour. A bird? Maybe a chaffinch? The sound of her steps were dampened and she could hear more little voices calling back and forth around her. She stopped still to catch a better look at the birds. Eventually one of the flashes settled. Just round the side of a tree in front. She leaned slowly to catch a look and sucked in her breath.

It. That. It couldn't be.

Whatever it was, it was no bird. It was barely as big as a ruler, but had arms and legs and big colourful wings, like thick butterfly wings. It was smooth and pale, and didn't have any clothes on. Doesn't it get cold, she couldn't help thinking.

She turned slowly to look around. More (were they really fairies, actual fairies?) things were settling in the branches. She was in a forest surrounded by actual, really real, fairies. She pinched herself just in case. No-one would ever believe her. This was amazing though, like all her prayers for a proper adventure had been answered. Just like in the storybooks. Little children got lost in the fairy forest and were guided back home.

These fairies weren't like the story ones though, nor the ones in her favourite flower fairy books. Their eyes were too large and their mouths too small to look like little people. Their noses were really just flat nostrils and their pointed ears lay close to their wispy hair. She shifted underneath their silent gazes. Ok, someone do something already. It was like that uncomfortable feeling when she was made to stand in the middle of the circle when they used to play Farmers in His Den. Everyone watching her and nowhere to hide from their attention.

If the stories were right then they'd help her, right? Show her the way out of this forest, however she had got here.

She took some tentative steps towards some of them, holding out her hand like she'd been taught to do with frightened animals.

"Hello," she said softly. There was a scurry and flurry of chirrups as most of the creatures hid. She took a breath; there were a couple of fairies still warily peering at her so she took another slow step towards them. "I won't hurt you. My name is Clare, I'm lost." The two fairies blinked and tilted their heads at her.

"Could you, could you maybe help me get home?"

The fairies turned to each other and then seemed to be having a whispered conversation with some others still half hidden behind the branch. One hop-fluttered over onto on a closer branch and looked at her with what was presumably a smile. It nodded and gestured happily to her to follow. Three others clambered into view looking more nervous. She looked back over her shoulder and saw that the others were still trying to hide from her. As she turned back, the 'lead' fairy stopped the gesturing it was doing at the others and again smiled and waved for her to follow. She felt her heart flutter. For a second it had looked almost, angry.

Shaking her head, she followed the little group. They hopped and fluttered along, like they couldn't fly as such, more like the wings helped them jump a lot further.

"Shouldn't we be going back the other way?" she asked. "The way I came?"

The fairies carried on without acknowledging her. She followed helplessly. There had to be an end to it at some point, right? No point being a downer, and what an adventure. She'd got to meet real live fairies, better than those girls with the photos. She could be famous, be on Blue Peter and the news.

She kept her eyes on them, skipping occasionally to catch up. They didn't seem to want to wait for her and she didn't want to get even more lost. After a while she noticed a distinct lack of birds or other animal sounds. Were they going deeper into the woods? She swallowed sickly, her stomach starting to ache. Her feet hurt and clouds of floating fluffy seeds were starting to make her eyes itch. She'd had enough and really wanted to go home now. It might already be mid-afternoon. Mum would be expecting her home before four, in time for her favourite TV. She stopped and rubbed her eyes.

"How much further?" she said, unable to keep the whine out of her voice. The fairies just chirruped at her, the lead one gesturing onwards. She saw from behind her hands the other fairies whispering to each other, casting looks her way. She was hit with a nasty jolt. She knew that look.

Abigail had once come over to her in the playground and asked her to be part of their group. She'd been thrilled to finally be in with the popular girls. The TV shows were right, she'd misjudged them and everyone could be friends if she gave them a chance. So she'd thrown herself into being the best friend she could be, doing whatever tasks they'd made up for her to do to keep their friendship. Kept smiling and laughing with them even when she always seemed to be the butt of their jokes, told herself she was just being over sensitive about the way the others snickered at her from the sidelines while Abigail ordered her around. Until the day after when she'd tried to join them at playtime and they'd laughed at her and asked why on earth she was coming over, and said to stop following them around like a puppy, she wasn't part of their group. Embarrassment and anger had burned on her cheeks as she walked away across the playground, alone again. She'd hidden at break times for the rest of the day, unable to face their mocking looks and cruel smiles. She swore she'd never be that stupid again, to believe someone like that wanted to be friends.

The fairies weren't helping her, they were mocking her. She wasn't going home at all. So much for the fairy tales. She should have known better than to trust them. She stopped still. The fairies took a moment to realise she wasn't following them anymore before chirruping at her again.

"No."

Their gestures got more insistent.

"No ! I'm not going any further." She could see the smiling act start to slip as the chirruping changed tone. Oh, how she recognized that tone.

"I know what you are. I know you're lying to me." She clenched her fists. "I don't need you. I'll find my own way home. Go away!"

The fairies bared their teeth at her, little needle sharp things. She quickly snapped a branch off and waved it at them. "Stay back or I'll smash you!" They hissed but backed away. "See," she said with a snarl. "I knew you were too good to be true. Horrible nasty two-faced little...cows," she spluttered. She gathered herself then screamed at the top of her lungs and stamped her foot towards them, waving the branch again for good measure. They skittered up a tree, hissing and spitting.

She turned and ran and ran. He eyes were tearing. She scrubbed at her face. It was the stupid fluff, that was all. She didn't care about ugly little fairies. Ha! Just wait until she told everyone they were wrong about them.

Just as soon as she found her way back. Oh yeah. Now what was she going to do? She bent over, huffing and catching her breath.

She turned a full circle. The trees surrounding her gave no clue if there was an edge to The Forest at all. What if it just went on forever? She shook her head. No, that was impossible. She just had to figure out which way to go. The sun was too obscured to be of any help, not that she could really remember how you were supposed to navigate by it. Nor stars either. She shivered. She did not want to still be here at night, when it was dark. So. Pick a direction. Away from those horrible fairies was a good start. Keep walking and hope something changes.

She really wanted to sit down and rest, though. A drink, a drink would be good too. Her tongue was sticking to the roof of her mouth. There was colour all around her, beautiful scenery. It was empty though, just a pretty picture. Not the truth. Everything was deathly quiet. She didn't like it. Where was everyone – no animals, not even horrible sneaky little creatures. Were there other children in here?

She stumbled as a loud roar rumbled through the forest. She was put in mind of a bear, a really big bear. Or maybe a dinosaur. She always had bad dreams about dinosaurs chasing her. A shock ran through her, like when someone snuck up and dumped cold water over you. This wasn't a dream. She found herself already running. It came again, and she could feel it through her feet. There were crashes as if it was tearing the forest apart. How close? If she turned around, would she be able to see it? Her neck prickled. She leapt and sprinted blindly through the trees, anywhere just away, until her lungs burned. She threw herself behind a tree, panting.

Strong enough to smash a tree. She'd been right about the old fallen trunk all along. Now she desperately wished she'd never noticed. She didn't want to know, didn't want to see.

Was it closer or further away? She couldn't tell over the thudding in her ears. She squeezed her eyes shut and sank down. Please, please, go away. Not real, not real, she pleaded. Was it wishful thinking or was it fainter? She felt weak all over, she should hide better, but couldn't move. Just clenched her legs together and prayed.

It could have been minutes, it could have been hours. Her mind was too scattered, but eventually it faded off into the distance. She opened her eyes and stared hopelessly at the unchanging mass of trees.

If she moved would it suddenly appear again? The stifling silence descended again. Almost as bad. When she had a bad dream, she'd lie as still as a statue until she could work up enough of a voice to yell for her mum and dad. But they weren't going to come this time, were they? No matter how loud she shouted. What would her parents do if she never made it home? She was so stupid.

She could do this. Jump up and start running, don't look back. Here she went. Any moment now. No really, she was going to do it, this time. With a whimper, she pushed up on shaky legs and leapt out of her hiding place like a rabbit. Her heart felt like it was in her throat, her skin stretched taught and screaming. Keep going, don't stop. You can outrun this. The initial burst of fear ran out quickly and she nearly went over on her ankle. She collapsed in a shivering heap.

This wasn't what everyone promised, this wasn't a magical place. Nothing was better here, there was no adventure, just a trap. There was no way out, was there? The forest just went on and on.

She wanted to go home. She scrunched her eyes closed and wanted and wanted. Let me go home. She didn't know who she was asking. She'd already tested God years ago and found him wanting. Just another story. The creatures here were no friends, that was for sure. If anyone would get her home though, she'd believe in them with everything she had.

Home. She'd stumble through the door, and Mum would offer her a snack before tea. She'd sit in front of the TV until Dad walked through the door, the metallic smell of the factory clinging to his suit. He'd ask her about her day and she'd shrug her shoulders and say it was boring; he'd laugh and then disappear to go have serious adult conversation with Mum while she cooked. Later, she'd moan about being made to go to bed while it was too light. The injustice of hearing other kids still playing out. Why was Mum so strict? She'd guilt Dad into reading her a story even though she was a big girl and could read a book in a day by herself. And wasn't that so unfair? Couldn't she stay in the time when she wasn't always told that, and there was always bedtime stories and no homework, or school? Where she didn't have to deal with stupid, so-called friends. She'd go to sleep dreaming of great futures for herself and when she woke up it would be another long summer day to fill on her own. So please, just let her find her way home.

She opened her eyes and her breath hitched. The familiar gate in the low whitewashed wall was in front of her. Her front path the same wobbly paving stones, the patchy grass, the slightly peeling front door. She'd wished, and here it was. Home. Safety.

And she knew. She knew if she went inside it would look exactly like home. The same smell, her toys exactly where she'd left them. She could run straight upstairs and onto her bed, pull the duvet over her head and never come out. Close her eyes and wish it all away. There might even be her mum in there, to give her a hug and tell her she was being silly. Would she look the same though? Would her eyes be the same? This other mother? Or would they be alien and cold like the fairies?

Her eyes burned with tears and her face crumpled. This wasn't fair. She couldn't face this forest anymore, she wanted home and everything that meant. If she went in there though, it wouldn't help. Why was everything so cruel here? Why couldn't there be a proper fairy tale ending?

"I hate you all," she whispered. "I hate your

empty lies, and your cruel jokes. I just want things to be fair and kind, is that too much to ask?" She took shuddering breaths; her throat ached from swallowed sobs. God she was so weak, just like they all said. No wonder no one wanted to be around her. So pathetic.

Well, screw you all. Maybe she was pathetic but she was still smarter. She could see through all the stories and lies now. Grief twisted to anger, the bitterness tasted sweet to her raging mind. Enough.

"I am going home," she said calmly, "and you won't stop me. I don't need you, I don't want you. You can't give me what I want. No one can." Another sharp ache in her throat. Breathe it away.

"I don't believe in you. Not anymore. I shall find my own way out."

She could, she knew she could. She just had to remember where The Wood was, where she'd been before. She imagined the cool breeze, the crunch of the leaves under her feet, the heat of the sun on her face as she stepped out onto the bare hill. Her hand crept into her pocket, and she rubbed soothing circles around her stone treasure

Closing her eyes, she took a deep breath. Yes, she could smell it, feel it. She turned towards it, a faint tickle against her face. She took a step forward, then another. Her foot fell further than it should. Lurching, like when she missed a step on the stairs. Wobbling, she opened her eyes - and blinked heavily against the sunlight in front of her.

She was back near the old trunk. She looked around in disbelief. The trees had thinned out again. She could see the edge and the familiar curve of the hill. It barely seemed much later than when she'd gone in.

With a lightness under her feet, she started running.

She didn't stop as the half-flew down the hill. She didn't stop as she ran through the still baking pavements of the new estate. She didn't stop as she caught glimpses of people who had ventured back out into their gardens now the worst of the day had passed. She was probably just a blur of pounding feet to them.

The smooth tarmac gave way to uneven paving slabs, and she was back on more familiar streets. Ones burnt into her memory. Turn at the lampost, cross the street, hold your breath under the laburnum (Mum had once said it was poisonous). As the street curved, look out for the monkey puzzle tree. One more turn and there it was. Home, her real home this time. She ran round the side of the house, and threw herself through the back door, making her mother jump in shock.

"Claire! You nearly gave me a heart attack."

She buried herself wordlessly into that familiar scent.

"What's got into you?"

Claire shook her head. "Nothing." She couldn't meet her mum's eyes, and still hide what she'd seen. "I'm going upstairs!" She dodged round her.

"Not in your shoes!" came her mum's admonishment, as she was already kicking them off, letting them bump down the stairs.

"I know!"

There it was, her bedroom just as she'd left it. Ted in the exact place on her bed, like nothing had changed. She picked him up and sniffed, rubbing his cool threadbare body against her cheek. She felt the remaining tension seep out of her. If Ted was the same, it was real.

"Claire, if you're back, you can help me get the washing in," her mum called up. For once Claire didn't complain.

Standing out there in silent companionship, the click and clatter of the pegs as they pulled them off into the box, she felt all the words buried just under her skin, ready to tumble out, but she held them back. This – thing - that had happened, it was hers, to know and keep. Something she somehow knew she'd never be able to explain to her mother, in a way she'd understand. She looked up. A few tiny clouds were sneaking in to break up the endless blue, the swifts had dropped a little lower, enough to see the scimitar shape of their wings. She could hear other birds now, and the bushes and trees were alive with bees and butterflies.

"Hey, daydreamer, I thought you were helping?"

Later, as Claire lay on her stomach watching the TV, she found her mind skipping about like those butterflies. The characters seemed like they were speaking from a distance. It all felt a bit flat.

Dad came home, and they ate tea without much difference, perfectly, strangely, normal.

Afterwards, she wandered into the garden. The paving stones were still warm under her feet, the birds were in full evening chorus. More clouds were joining in the sky, but it still felt far too hot for the time of evening. She kicked a ball against the side of the house, enjoying the echoey boing it made. Her rhythmic counting was soothing.

The light was going down. She looked up at the sky and it was a dirty pink. Everything felt heavy. She realised the birds had stopped singing. Her heart lurched and she froze. A breeze ruffled at her hair. Then, a distant rumble. She took a relieved breath. Thunder.

A last group of birds made a mad dash across the sky, ahead of the storm clouds now looming. Another rumble, and the breeze picked up. It felt wonderful. Big, fat drops began to fall. Her mother called her in, so she watched from the door as the rain came down in sheets. The house seemed to vibrate with the sound in between huge flashes. She stayed until her mother clucked at her letting the rain in, and shooed her up to bed. She lay there as the flashes lit up her room through the curtains, and counted between rumbles that felt like they were coming down the chimney. Until they got further and further apart, and the rain pattered to a stop. Her eyes were heavy. Tomorrow everything would be fresh and new, the day washed away. There was no one she could tell. No one who would understand anyway. It was something scary and precious she would keep to herself. Maybe one day she'd find the right person to share it with, someone who could *see* the same as her. One day. It was okay, she was good at waiting.

She curled round herself, hugging her secrets tight, and let sleep come.

About the Contributors

MEGAN ELIZABETH ALLEN lives in St. Louis, Missouri, with her two cats and her best friend. She teaches Environmental Writing at a local college, having earned her PhD in English Literature, but she grew up in rural Arkansas, where she learned how to hunt and fish and make sassafras tea.

LH ANNABLE, once an academic, is now a self employed creative person and runs her own craft business by day. She's also passionate about writing and reading, and a lifelong fan of all things fantastical and horrifying, though only in literature, she hastens to add. She has been writing creatively for nearly two decades and has discovered two things. One, it never gets any easier and two, there can never be enough tea.

CATHRYN BURGE has been a writer for most of her life, apart from the decade she tried being a Serious Grownup, and even then, she kept rats and wrote stories in her head about aliens and vampires.
Originally from Bristol, she lives in Glasgow with her family and hyperactive dog. She has a degree in French and has taken courses in Creative Writing and Screenwriting. Cathryn taught French and English before becoming a translator and editor. She plays the piano (hilariously), draws (ambitiously) and sometimes bakes. Her gardening skills are limited to the occasional foray with her savage secateurs.

EKATERINA FAWL was born is Siberia and currently lives in Manchester. While her background is in Economics, Finance and Computing, writing has been her life-long passion. She's been a member of Manchester Speculative Fiction writing group almost since its conception. Her short stories were published in Daily Science Fiction Year Two Anthology and Revolutions Anthology. She's a guest blogger at the Writing Tree working on a series of post about writing communities and the art of giving and receiving feedback.

HELEN KENWRIGHT writes hopeful speculative fiction in novel and short story form. She has an MA with distinction in Creative Writing from York St John University, and is the Director and founder of the Writing Tree. She also works as a creative writing tutor for Converge, a project at York St John University which offers educational opportunities for people who use mental health services. Helen lives in York with two cats and plays more video games than generally expected for a woman of her age. You can find her on Twitter @hnkenwright and at her website, www.helenkenwright.com

SUSI LIARTE is a multilingual writer and artist. She loves fantasy worlds and speculative fiction, and is currently working on several short stories as well as a novel. She has an MA in Translation Studies and is interested in languages, creativity and technology. She writes best to music, preferably with a large mocha nearby.

K J LOWE's childhood was spent with a head full of stories and learning the names of all the types of clouds. Despite her best efforts however, she never met any fairies. This is her first published work with thanks to the the support of the wonderful members of The Writing Tree.

EMMALYN SPARK enjoys writing, fairytales, reading, cakes and ice hockey, not necessarily in that order. She has a short story forthcoming from Nine Star press and is currently studying for an MA in creative writing. You can find her at @EmmalynnSpark on twitter.

Cover art '*Storymaker*' by TG of RainDragon Arts.

About the Writing Tree

The Writing Tree is an organisation dedicated to the support and nurturing of creative writers. Founded in 2011, the Writing Tree offers one-to-one tuition, coaching and editing services and range of online and community courses.

The guiding principles of the Writing Tree are that creative writing has importance independent of subject, purpose or audience, and that everyone has the right to write, and to write what they wish.

This book is the first publication for the Writing Tree Press.

You can find us online at www.writingtree.co.uk, on Twitter (@writing_tree), where we offer daily prompts for writing, and on Facebook (@WritingTree) and Tumblr (writingtree).

Acknowledgements

This, the very first publication by Writing Tree Press, would not have been possible without the commitment, creativity and encouragement of SFUK over the years, or the specific support and cheerleading for this project from Mim Evferstedt, Stephanie Hardy, Nik Wilcox and Ciaran Roberts and all the contributors, who looked after each other brilliantly. Thank you.

Many thanks to Faye Allison and Ciaran Roberts for proofing and feedback, and to the production team: Susi, Katya, Cath and Tanzie.

And, always, to Ste Kenwright, who always believed in me, and us, and squee. To the stars and back, Captain.

Printed in Poland
by Amazon Fulfillment
Poland Sp. z o.o., Wrocław